HOMELESS

Karl D. Keen

Author's Tranquility Press
ATLANTA, GEORGIA

Copyright © 2024 by Karl D. Keen

All rights reserved. No part of this publication may be reproduced, distributed or transmitted in any form or by any means, including photocopying, recording, or other electronic or mechanical methods, without the prior written permission of the publisher, except in the case of brief quotations embodied in critical reviews and certain other noncommercial uses permitted by copyright law. For permission requests, write to the publisher, addressed "Attention: Permissions Coordinator," at the address below.

Karl D. Keen/Author's Tranquility Press
3900 N Commerce Dr. Suite 300 #1255
Atlanta, GA 30344, USA
www.authorstranquilitypress.com

Ordering Information:
Quantity sales. Special discounts are available on quantity purchases by corporations, associations, and others. For details, contact the "Special Sales Department" at the address above.

Homeless / Karl D. Keen
Library of Congress Control Number:2024921485
Hardback: 978-1-965075-60-9
Paperback: 978-1-965075-57-9
eBook: 978-1-965075-58-6

Dedication

To my wife Virginia,
without whose help this book would not have been
possible.

Though based on a true story, the character names and places mentioned in this book are purely fictional.

CHAPTER I

I sat huddled in front of the empty building, watching the traffic creep along Karney Street. The white fog trailing from the auto exhaust gave notice to the cold in the air. My main concern was how I was going to stay warm through the coming night. I was hungry and knew I could get a soup and sandwich at the mission, just down the block. They also had a few beds if you could stand the smell of all the other souls like me, that hadn't bathed too often. Hell! I hadn't bathed in weeks and I didn't care. I had long become accustomed to my own smell. It was winter and the clothes I had on had an odor of their own; a lot of wood and coal smoke from sitting around a fire, down in the hobo jungle behind the old Frisco yards. I smelled the cheap wine I drank to hold off the cold of the night before. My stomach was still soured from the after effect; I could taste the bile in my throat. I knew with each swallow I was getting sicker by the moment. I hadn't eaten all day and it was well past noon. I would now have to wait until the evening soup at the mission or try to con up enough money from some passing stranger. Not many people walked along Karney Street now, as it was mostly homeless, and the downtrodden people like myself that had given up on society. Most of the good people of Springdale looked down on us as lazy dirty people that had no purpose for living. They saw us as too damn lazy to work, or try to work, and bring ourselves up out of the gutter that we had sunk into.

I felt the retched bile of vomit coming up from my stomach, as I tried to get to the alley behind the closed-out store. I knew if I became sick out on the sidewalk, and the cops came by, I would be put in the tank with ever other sick, crazy, stinking derelict that was picked up that night. I couldn't face spending another twenty-four hours in there again. Most of the officers on the force had some compassion for us, but they had their rules to go by just like everyone else. I had conned my way out of going to the tank several times, and knew it was just a matter of time before I was labeled as a regular. Then I would be picked up every time I was seen. I would then have to move to another location or town.

A lot of the police tried to ignore us, as they didn't like the way we smelled and didn't want us in their patrol cars. We were just another daily problem to them. I really couldn't blame them, even in my state of mind, I could relate to what had happened to me. I guess it is pride that keeps me on the street; if you can believe a person that has stooped this low could still have some pride. I am just trying to survive. For what, I don't know. I'm just taking it one miserable day at a time. I have grown to distrust everyone. Every day I see people I know, but they seem to be embarrassed to know me. Maybe I have hit them up for a hand-out before, and they are afraid I will again. I can't remember half the things I did while on the wine, or pills, when I could get them. The VA has cut me off all my regular pills as I abused them with alcohol and any other thing, I could find to mix with it to ease the misery of living on the street. I have to keep my mind in a stupor to keep the painful memories out. I look at other people here on the street and wonder what fate in life put them here.

The wave of sickness soon passed. I was sweating from the dry heaves now and knew I would soon be that much colder. I had to find a place to spend the night as the temperature was falling fast and it would soon be dark. If I could get to the smoke stack behind the hospital maybe I could wedge in between it and the building and get the heat from the bricks. It was out in the open, but it didn't look like it would rain or snow this night. I have given up on eating, and I haven't any money for food or drink anyway. I just want a warm place to spend the night, only it is ten or more blocks to the back of the hospital. I hope no one else is back there. I walk as fast as possible trying not to draw attention from the passing patrol cars. I know they are watching me, wondering where I will pick a place to crash for the night.

The parking lot behind the hospital is nearly empty, and there is only one car in the alley by the smoke stack. As I try to slip into the void between the building and the stack, a man calls out to me and asks what I am doing back there. I tell him I am just trying to get warm. He asked me to come into the boiler room, which is located back of the smoke stack, saying, "You can get warm in here." As I follow him into the warm room I can see the two huge boilers, with their coal fires roaring. I can feel the heat from them clear out by the door. He offered me a chair and asked me to sit down and rest awhile.

He takes a large thermos and pours a cup of hot coffee and hands it to me. I have never tasted anything so good as that coffee tasted at that moment. I had not eaten all day and my stomach was a mess from the wine and pills of the night before. Opening his lunch box, he offered me an egg sandwich of which he had two. He said he never ate but one anyway. That his wife always packed two and he usually feeds one to the cats that prowl the alleys around the hospital. We sat and ate in silence, soaking up the heat radiating from the boilers. After a while he arose, and shoving the lunch pail under the chair, told me to help myself to more coffee, as he got it free in the hospital.

He picked up a long steel rod with a bend on the end. Walking to the boiler, he reached into the red-hot fire and started pulling hunks of red-hot coal toward the front. He said he had to keep the clinkers pulled out, or they would foul up the draft system, and the boilers would smoke. Had to keep room for new coal to be added. Taking a long-handled shovel, he lifted the hunks of red and black hot coals from the furnace and laid them on the cement floor to cool. Said he had to do this about every two hours; each time before shoveling in more coal.

Turning to a large bin of coal stacked on the side, he lifted several large shovels full of coal and pitched it into the roaring fire.

Turning to the next furnace, he repeated the same process, sweat popping out on his face each time he moved back from the fire. He told me to sit tight, as he had to go check the heat risers and thermostats on the blowers in the hospital. I had finally gotten warm, and the sandwich had settled my stomach. I poured another cup of coffee, and sitting back I thought, this had been the first time I had been warm since spending a night in the mission, three days before. I was going to sit there as long as I could for I knew a cold miserable night lay ahead of me.

This man had befriended me and I had not even asked him his name! Maybe there were still a few people who cared in this world. I knew I should be gone before he returned, and just as I got up to leave, he came through the door. I told him goodbye. He asked if I had a place to stay. I told him I had planned on sleeping behind the stack. He said I could sleep behind the boiler until he got off work at four a.m.

Thanking him, I moved in behind the furnace and was asleep in minutes. In a daze, I could hear him scraping the coal from the floor and removing more spent coal remains from the furnace. At least I was warm and not hungry for a while.

Only too soon I heard him holler. "You will have to leave before my relief gets here." This man gave me two dollars, and with a wink said, "Don't spend it on wine." I thanked him and stepped out into the bitter cold. The force of the cold wind made me wince with pain. God, I would have loved to go back in behind that boiler.

I walked behind the building and wedged in close to the stack. My mind turned to Mary and the baby girl I had never seen. I tried to fight off the memory, but it kept haunting me. No matter how hard I tried to think of other things, her memory kept returning. The cold was getting to me now. I shook violently as I tried to get to a warmer side of the stack. I wondered where Mary would be, was she still in the state? Or had she taken our daughter and moved away? Was she warm and secure? These thoughts kept returning. I had never even found out what the baby's name was. She was born while I was in Nam. The car by the stack started up and drew me out of my thoughts. It was the man that had given me coffee, and a warm place. He looked old and tired as he backed out and pulled away. I wondered how far he had to go to get to a warm house and a nice warm bed. It had been so long since I had slept in a good home, I couldn't remember.

The cold kept chilling me through the heavy Army coat I wore. I shook violently and wondered how long it would be until the coffee at the mission was served. I could always get a meal there, but first I would have to sit and listen to someone talk to us about Jesus.

I have a fairly good belief in God, even though I can't understand how he could let some things happen. I sure didn't need some want to-be preacher telling me stuff I really didn't believe, just to get a bowl of lumpy oatmeal and some dried-out toast. I couldn't take the cold much longer. Then I remembered the two dollars the man had given me. There was a little all-night dinner over on Division Street, where I could get a cup of coffee for twenty cents.

I stayed by the smoke stack for a few more minutes then decided I needed to move or freeze. As I trudged up Kearny Street, headed for Division, I could see several other homeless people bundled up in alleys and doorways, trying to ward off the bitter cold. A patrol car drove by me real slow and looked me over good. Then sped off at a high rate of speed. Probably missed his doughnut break! I thought to myself. I was several blocks from the diner and I was shaking violently from the cold, and probably hunger. Even though I didn't feel hungry after the sandwich I had eaten earlier. Once you have been on the streets and get real hungry a time or two, I guess your stomach shrinks, as you never seem to get really hungry again.

As I turned the corner and headed toward the diner, I could see someone lying in a doorway of an empty building with a half-empty bottle of wine by him. I helped myself to the bottle, as I was shaking from the need of alcohol as well as the cold. I drank down the bitter, vinegar-tasting cheap wine. The patrol car slowed down and stopped beside me, and I knew I was going to be hassled again. Maybe even thrown in the tank. I stood there with the empty bottle in my hand, shaking from the bitter cold, but the cheap wine had started to warm me a little. The officer asked where I was headed, I told him to the diner for breakfast "What are you going to do steal it?" he asked.

I wanted to hit the smart bastard with the bottle, but I just smiled and said, "I still have a few bucks left."

His radio came on with something I didn't understand. He drove off answering another call, I guess, leaving me there in the cold.

The diner was empty except for one old man and a skinny waitress, who looked like she had been through more hell than me. I slid into a corner booth and sat there for a long time before she asked if I wanted to order something. "Just coffee," I said. She acted like it hurt her to move, and I suppose being on her feet all night it probably did.

The coffee was hot and bitter. I poured it full of sugar, as I need the calories, even though I preferred it black.

There was a quarter and two pennies behind the sugar container. I took the two pennies and left the quarter for the coffee. I sat there drinking coffee for as long as I could, as there were few customers coming in at this hour, and no one was paying any attention to me. It was nearing eight o'clock when I left the diner.

I walked on toward Commercial Street, knowing that the Brown Derby liquor store would open at nine. The cold was still miserable and I moved as quick as I could.

The bus depot was just up the street, and I slipped in through the side door and went into the rest room before anyone saw me. The manager had thrown me out of there on several occasions; after I had tried to spend a night sleeping in out of the cold.

I used the facilities and washed up the best I could. Paper towels make a poor washcloth. I didn't have a comb. I hated looking into a mirror. I had become severely disfigured while in Nam. The VA hospital had done what they could for me, but the injuries were totally out of their realm of miracles. I pulled the stocking cap down over my blind left eye and scarred-up ear, realizing just how terrible I looked. It was the first time I had taken a good look at myself in several weeks. It made me sick inside. How could anyone stand to look at me? How could God allow this to happen to anyone?

I sat in a stall of the rest room for what seemed like an hour or more. Leaving, I slipped out the side door without the manager even seeing me. It was spitting snow now and the cold had let up some; the wind was gone. It was just a cold, damp, miserable day.

People were moving along the streets now, and the vehicle traffic was in the morning rush. I crossed the street and went into the liquor store. Picking up two bottles of Thunder Bird wine, I placed them on the counter.

The clerk said, "That will be a dollar thirty-eight," as he placed each bottle in a brown sack and twisted the top. He handed me my change, and picking up the bottles, I left heading for the jungle behind the Frisco yard.

There were few trains in the Frisco yard as I walked across the many tracks. The yard bulls watched me close, making sure I didn't slip into a boxcar. I crossed over behind the roundhouse and through a drainage tunnel, out into the jungle of berry vines and poison ivy. I could see several men standing by a fire they had going from pieces of old railroad ties. The black smoke was curling skyward. They only glanced at me and kept talking among themselves.

"Care if I share the heat?" I asked.

"Come on in," came a reply. I stood there for a moment. Taking one of the bottles from my pocket, I loosened the cap and took a long drink; every eye was on me. I passed the bottle to the next person and it made its round; as it got back to me there was only a drink left in it so I gave it to an older man who was standing shaking by the fire. He smiled and drank down the last of the wine. "Thank you," he said, smiling through rotten and missing teeth.

I stayed there by the fire until well into the late afternoon; the snow had continued to fall lightly all day and the ground was now white with a fine skiff of powdered snow. My thoughts were on where I could spend this night. I still had a full fifth of wine, which would keep me in a stupor and from feeling the cold. I had spent several nights under the skating rink at the park. They stored carnival rides under there during the winter months and some of the seats were quite large. By pulling some of the canvas over the seats I could make a comfortable bed, and the wine would keep me warm for the night. I walked to the park, waiting for it to get dark so I could slip under the rink without being seen.

After dark, I slipped along the side of the building until I came to a small screen-covered opening. Pulling back the screen, I slipped under the rink. I could hear the roar of the skate wheels on the floor as the skaters made the circles around the rink. I knew that this would all end in a couple of hours. I felt my way along the rides until I found the seats of the caterpillar ride. They were about six-feet wide and padded. Crawling in, I pulled the canvas cover down around me, and was cold, but comfortable. I hadn't eaten all day and knew the wine would take effect quickly, so pulling the cap I took a long drink. Upon hitting my empty stomach, it almost came back up.

I lay there listening to the skaters and sipping on the wine. I don't know when the skaters left, but when I awoke it was daytime. I was stiff and shaking violently from the cold. I still had over a half bottle of wine, so I drained a lot of it in one long drink. I lay there wondering how I could get from under the building without being seen. Stashing what was left of the wine, I crawled to the opening, and seeing no one around, I crawled out to meet the day.

I knew I needed to eat a good meal soon or my stomach was going to be in trouble. I headed for Division Street and the mission. I was cold and with the new snow I knew I would get colder, so the mission and the lesson about Jesus didn't seem too bad. There were very few people on the streets; I guess the snow kept everyone home. Hell, I wish I had a home. I wonder what one would feel like, after spending all these months on the street, and a year in the jungles of Nam? I couldn't remember much about a home. Then the sickening thoughts of Mary came back. God, how I had loved her! How could she do me like she did? And Artie, my best friend, moving in on my wife and family while I was in Nam. I should have killed him and her too. But I have seen enough killing to last me for a lifetime.

The mission wasn't too crowded, and the Jesus talking was about over when I arrived. So I sat and talked to Bob, the want-to-be preacher that ran the mission. The coffee was good and hot; so was the oatmeal, and the toast was fresh. For a change, we even had fresh-made doughnuts. Wonder where the cops are?

Bob knew me from previous visits, and we talked for several hours. It was warm and comfortable in the mission. I felt good with the warm food. Bob even offered me the use of the mission 's shower, which I accepted. He even washed my clothes while I was in the shower, giving me an old robe to wear until my clothes were dry. He gave me clean underwear, and some new fatigue clothes that the VA had given him. I had to admit it felt good to be clean again. I helped Bob clean up the mission and asked if I could spend the night. He asked me what my plans were.

I said, "To stay alive another day. Just like in Nam, all I asked God for was just one more day. Anyway, the way I look no one is going to give me a job. Hell, I scared the shit out of half the people that ever took a good look at me. It makes me want to puke when I look in a mirror. I have never even gone to see my own mother since I've returned. I wonder if she is still alive?"

Bob placed a hand on my shoulder and. said, "Yes, she is still alive. She always asks me about you, every Sunday when I see her. She begs me to have you come and see her. She is in a rest home over on Bartlet Street. I preach a sermon for them every Sunday afternoon. Why don't you come with me?"

"No, Bob! I don't think so! Hell, one look at me and those old people would die by the dozen. I would never want Mom to see me like this. It is better she remembers me like I used to be. This wound cost me my wife and daughter, too, so it is better this way. I could never fit into a family; everyone would be uncomfortable around me and the children would be scared of me. I can see it in their eyes when we pass on the streets. The parents turn away after one look and try to shield the kids from me like I am some pervert. Even the homeless people on the street shy away from me. I can see the pity in their eyes when they look at me. But I am better off than a lot of the boys that came back from that damn war. At least I can still walk and hear and talk. It is the feelings that kill me. I still have sexual urges. I still need a woman. I am still capable of love. I still need to be loved and to be able to love someone. But no woman alive could stand to look at me, without anything but pity. I don't want their damn pity. I just want to be a man. To look normal and feel normal, whatever that is. The wine and pills kill some of the pain, and it is killing me also. Some days I think it can't come fast enough. I would end it myself, but I made a deal with God; if he would let me live through Nam, then I would never take another life. The next day I was wounded and I wish I had never made that deal. I came back from Nam a damn freak.

"Bob, I don't know what to do. There are surgeons that could build me a new face, if I had the money. The VA just doesn't do cosmetic surgery, all they do is patch some poor miserable bastard like me up and send him out to scare the hell out of the world. There is many a man out there on the street that is scarred up on the inside a damn sight worse than I am on the outside. We take these young men from their mothers and put them through a hell that most people can't even visualize. God, Bob, let's talk about something else. How do you do this all the time? How do you keep from going insane? I know faith in God is strong, but there are limits to what a person can take. "We talked until long after midnight. And Bob gave me a cot in a room by myself. Come morning I needed a drink bad, and Bob could tell. He poured a shot from a bottle of whiskey he had, which I took with joy, even though it did surprise me that he would have that stuff around.

"It is medicine for the soul," he said. "Some of the people couldn't eat without a shot first. You can't heal the soul while the body suffers." I helped Bob serve the breakfast toast and oatmeal, but skipped the Jesus lecture and chose to do the dishes instead. This didn't go unnoticed by Bob, however, and we talked about it after everyone left.

"Do you believe in God?" he asked.

"Yes, I do, but I don't believe in the things he lets happen to people. I believe that God has the right to give life and take life. But to put someone through what I and others on the street go through is purely from hell."

"And so it is," said Bob. "Maybe you are blaming the wrong person, or I should say source."

This went through my mind like a rocket. I needed to get out on the street where I could sort this out.

Leaving the mission, I headed toward Campbell Street and the post office where I shared a mailbox with my brother, whom I hadn't seen in over a year. Sometimes he left me a few bucks in an envelope and then I got my check from the VA on the third of each month. After the two hundred and fifty bucks went for child support of a daughter I had never been allowed to see, I got about four hundred and eighty-four dollars. I would always leave the money there to pay back Vick, but he would never take it, so it always ended up going for booze.

I didn't even know what day it was and wasn't too sure about the month. I just knew it was several weeks past Christmas, and a most miserable time of year. The postal box held a note and ten bucks from Vick. He asked how I was and again asked me to go see Ma. Vick was a good brother, but even he had a hard time looking at me. He would always talk to the ground when we met, and he could never make eye contact with me. He never offered to have me come to his home either. I believe he had two girls, but I never knew for sure. He was three years older than me. He had come to the hospital once in Maryland to see me, after I was wounded. One look and he was in shock. He left without ever saying goodbye.

HOMELESS

He had set up the postal box through Bob, at the mission, just in case I ever came in there. Then one day at the post office I met him coming out. We had a long talk about Mom and myself; only he could never look at me. He worked for a tax outfit in town and lived over on Van Owen somewhere. It was too far for me to walk and I hadn't driven in years. Even if I would have had something to drive, I would never have gone there anyway. I don't know who he married and don't know for sure about the children.

Anyway, I was glad for the ten dollars, as all I had was sixty-eight cents. I needed a drink and was trying to figure out how to get a penny, as wine was sixty-nine cents a fifth; also, it was getting late and I had no idea where to spend the night. The park was a good place, but it was clear across town from where I was. I stopped in at the Consumers Grocery on National and got a bottle of wine. I figured I would stop at the White Front Hamburger and get three of the little burgers they sold for a dollar. The snow had all melted and the sky was clear. I knew it would be cold, but not the bone-chilling cold of the nights before. As I left the White Front Burger, I decided to go over to the hospital and sleep by the stack.

I stopped at a little park on Grant Street and ate the burgers. I was sipping the wine from the bottle when the patrol car drove by. They circled the block and came back. I hid the bottle on top of the rest room building and walked toward the pool, knowing they couldn't drive over that way. The cops stopped and watched me for a while. I just waited by the pool fence until they left. I figured they wouldn't walk over there just to hassle me. As soon as they were gone, I retrieved the bottle and walked down the alley toward the hospital. It was getting cold now and my hands were freezing. I felt good except for the cold. The wine had warmed me up and the little burgers were good. I hated nights, hated to see them come, especially the winter nights. It was always such a hassle looking for a place to sleep.

I was hoping to see the boiler-fire man at the hospital. Maybe he would let me sleep behind the furnace until four again. His car was parked by the stack as before. I waited for him to wheelbarrow out some of the cold clinkers. After some time, the door to the boiler room opened, and he stood there smoking a cigarette. I walked up to talk. He seen me and said, "Good evening" before I could speak.

I said, "How are you doing?"

"Not too good," he said. "I am tired today, didn't get much sleep with all the kids home from school. Some kind of school holiday." "How many kids do you have?" I asked.

"Only twelve," he said. "All but four girls are gone from home now. I have eight girls and four boys. Come in and have some coffee and rest a spell. I need to fire up this other boiler and then I will be right with you." He poured me a cup of coffee and offered me a sandwich.

I said, "No thanks."

"Better eat it or the cats will get it. It is only a fried egg, but my old lady makes a damn good egg sandwich."

"OK, if you put it that way." And he was right. It was the best egg sandwich I ever ate; of course, I couldn't remember ever eating a fried egg sandwich before.

It wasn't long before the other furnace was roaring and the room was hot even with the big door open. He came over and sat at a little table and wrote down something.

"I have to keep records," he said. "Every time I start a furnace or clean one or shut down for any reason. I guess if the damn thing blows up, they want to know who started the fire in it."

We both laughed. He was a cheerful sort of a man in his late fifties, I guess. He pulled out his lunch box and ate a boiled egg and poured some coffee.

"Have your own chickens?" I asked "How can you tell? Just because I fed you egg sandwiches both times makes you suspicious, doesn't it?" he laughed, and said, "We have about twenty old hens, most don't lay very good."

He always looked directly at me when he talked. My looks didn't seem to bother him at all. It kind of made me uncomfortable. I wasn't used to having someone look at me.

"How did you get hurt?" he asked.

It took me off guard, as I didn't see this coming. "I was wounded in Viet Nam," I said.

"All four of my sons were in the Navy; the youngest is still in. On an aircraft carrier over there some place. He never tells us where he is. I don't know if it is against the rules or if he doesn't want to worry us. He flies in helicopters. He is an air crewman of some kind." I thought of the door gunners that raked fire over us to keep the Viet Kong off us while we were trying to load up and get out. Many times those men risked their own lives for us.

"He has a good job," I told him.

We sat in silence for a long time. After a while he asked, "Are you from around here?"

"Yes. I grew up on a farm over by Arco. I went to school there and played football and basketball. I got drafted the same summer I got out of school. I was married and could have gotten out of it, but I thought, what the hell, I would go and do my part. Dad lost the farm after I left. I got the hell shot out of me, and my best friend stole my wife and daughter while I was in Nam. I am sorry," I told him. "I didn't mean to spill all my troubles on you."

He got up. "It is all right. Let me clean the furnace and we will talk about it, if you want to." Taking the long poker, he pulled the red-hot coals from the fire. The sweat would break out on his forehead every time he moved back from the fire.

"It must be terribly hot down there."

"Not bad in the winter, but it is pure hell in the summer," he said. For some reason, I felt perfectly at ease with this man. I had not trusted anyone in a long time. I didn't even know his name, yet he seemed like someone I had known for years. I watched him clean the fires and add coal to them. He seemed old to me, too old to be working this hard, then I thought of my own father. The long hot days he spent plowing and working the fields, only to lose it all due to a drought and a bank that lost faith in his ability to farm. The man came back, opened his lunch pail, poured some more coffee, and ate the other egg sandwich. After he was finished, he looked at me, and said, "Now do you want to talk?" "What about?" I said.

"You, me, anything that is on your mind. Tell me about yourself. Who you are and how you got here. I don't even know your name. I am Albert," he said, sticking out his hand.

I shook his hand and said, "I am Danny! Danny Watts, most folks just call me Dan."

We sat and talked for a long time. He would get up and mess with the fire ever so often. I thought about what it would be like to have a job again. Was there some type of work I could do? I needed to be around someone, I had become so lonely out there on the street. I had become paranoid of most of the people on the street. I needed someone to need me. I needed a woman in the worst way. This man had become my friend, and someone to mentor me. I had to get off the street. He came back, sat down and we resumed our conservation.

CHAPTER II

I was born on a farm outside of Arco, Missouri. I grew up there with my brother Vick and a sister Viola. Vick is three years older than me, and Sis is two years younger. I went to grade school and high school in Arco. I grew up with Mary Wilson, who later became my wife. We started dating when I was a junior in high school. I always loved Mary long before I ever dated her. I would watch her in Sunday school and in class at school. She was the girl my dreams were made from.

I was a fair athlete at Arco. Not the greatest by any means, but big enough to hold my own. I was over six foot when I was a sophomore, sort of a skinny kid, but by my junior year I had started to fill out; by the time I was a senior I was over six-two and over two hundred pounds. I played end on the football team and forward on basketball. I never had the good moves it takes to be a good basketball player. Maybe it was because I watched Mary in her cheerleading uniform more than I did the ball. I never really wanted to be a pro ball player like a lot of kids. I just wanted to be a farmer like my dad. We farmed on four hundred and sixty acres. It was good ground for crops and pasture and we milked thirty head of cattle and raised most of the feed ourselves.

Vick never took to farming like I did. I loved the smells of new hay and cattle and liked to run machinery. Vick left for college at Columbia shortly after he got out of high school. Dad and I got along great; he rode me a little when I got too hot rodding the tractor or doing other stupid things. Mom and Sis seldom did any farm work other than the family garden and keeping care of the house. We never had a lot of fancy things, we ate well, and always had good vehicles to drive.

There was a little one-bedroom cabin on the farm, and during my senior year I asked Dad if I could fix it up. My grandparents had lived there before the big house was built. Dad asked if I was moving out to it, and I said yes, if Mary would marry me after school was out.

He said, "Boy, you better know what you are doing. Don't you plan on going to college like your brother?"

I said I was fed up with books and school; I wanted to stay and work on the farm. Maybe lease some ground from the neighboring places that were no longer in production.

Dad smiled at me and said, "Well, son, we will have to think this over and talk to Ma first. So don't go popping the question just yet." I had never really dated other girls much. My best friend Artie Johnson and I used to go over to Greenland and pick up two sisters that lived there. We had met them on a school trip to Lake of the Ozarks. They were fun to be with, but Mary was the only girl I ever wanted. Artie was a tall, blond, nice-looking kid that could have almost any girl he wanted. He was the quarterback on the football team, and I always believed he would play for some college someplace. He was by far the smartest kid in our school, and one of the best basketball players around.

I had talked to him about marrying Mary, and he said I was nuts to get married before I got out of college. I said, "I am not going."

"Good God, Danny! You have to go to college nowadays, or work in a damn feed mill all your life for two bucks an hour. What are you going to do?"

"I have several head of cattle of my own, and I can lease the farm next to us. By helping Dad I can use his machinery, until I can sell a crop or two."

"Big deal," he said. "Do you think that Mary is going to go for a life of living on a farm?"

"We have discussed living in the cabin for a few years and me working for Dad. I must admit she wasn't overjoyed by the idea, but she will come around. Heck, I haven't even asked her to marry me yet. She thinks she wants to go to nursing school, but she could still do that even after we are married. They have a good program at the Springdale Hospital."

"And what about kids? You know people living together seem to have them most of the time."

I said, "Artie, you worry about things too much. We will cross that bridge when we get to it."

The old man must have gotten tired of listening to me. He stood up and said, "I got to go check the registers inside. Make yourself comfortable, I will be back directly." With his clipboard, he walked out the door toward the back of the hospital. I moved in behind the furnace and lay on a bench that was built there. Sleep wouldn't come, though, as I kept thinking of Mary and my little girl. I could picture her snug in a nice warm bed with clean blankets and sheets, and a doll or teddy bear cradled in her arms while she slept.

I wondered if she had dark hair like me or was it light like her mother's? What color eyes did she have? What did

Mary ever tell her about her father, or was she assuming that someone else was her father? I had never thought Artie would do that to me. I knew he always had eyes for Mary, but we were best of friends, and friends just didn't do that to each other. Well, I sure as hell learned different, didn't I?

Soon the old man returned and began cleaning the hot clinkers out of the furnace. I finally drifted off to sleep with some weird dreams haunting me; I was back in Nam in some sleazy bar and the VC were after me. I couldn't seem to move. Then a hand touched me. I jumped half off the bench; it was Albert.

"My shift is up now," he said, "and my relief will be here pretty quick. It isn't too cold out this morning. Do you have money for breakfast?" he asked.

"Yeah, I am ok," I said. "I can help Bob over at the mission."

"Can I give you a ride over?" he asked.

"Well, if you're going that way, I would appreciate it."

He drove an older, blue Ford that ran pretty good; anyway, the heater worked. I knew the mission wouldn't open for a couple of hours yet. So I had him drop me off over at the diner on Division Street.

The same poor, old, skinny waitress was sitting at the counter smoking, and two other men were sitting in a booth eating breakfast.

"Want coffee, you know where the cups are," she said, without even looking up.

I served myself coffee. Then I decided to have a short stack, as I still had some money from what Vick had given me. She acted like it hurt her to move, as she took the order and turned it into the cook, who was an old toothless man with a short, unlit stub of a cigar hanging out of his mouth. It didn't look too sanitary, but who was I to complain. I hadn't had a bath since the night in the mission a week ago, and I am sure I didn't meet with their approval, with the old stocking cap pulled over my missing ear and half-gone eye. Hell, it would have made them puke up last night's supper if they had to take a good look at me.

My order came and she tried not to look as she sat it down in front of me. I looked up at her and winked with the only eye I had left. I could see the fear and pity in her face as she turned away. The hot cakes were real good, and the first I had had in several weeks. The coffee made me warm and sleepy, as I hadn't gotten much sleep, from spending half the night talking to Albert over at the hospital boiler room. I sat and dozed and sipped my coffee until after eight. I needed a drink bad, as I was starting to shake; the sugar from the hot cakes syrup was helping very little.

I stopped at Consumers Market and picked up two bottles of wine. Now I needed a sheltered place to sit and drink by myself. I walked over to the park on Grant Street. It was raining lightly and the wind was picking up. It was a cold east wind and I knew that snow could be coming with it. There was a park building where they stored picnic tables and large dumpsters. I walked over there, but the men were working in the open building, so I just walked on over to the railroad overpass on Chestnut. I could at least get out of the wind and rain by crawling up under the support structure.

HOMELESS

It wasn't too bad there; someone else had dragged a large cardboard carton up underneath and blocked off the wind. I sat there and drank the wine and thought about my life and wondered if I would be alive this time a year from now. My teeth were going bad and I had lost probably fifty pounds when I got out of the VA hospital. I wasn't eating the right food or enough of them. The wine had played hell with my nerves, and the Valium that the doctors had put me on didn't mix well with booze.

I was homeless and I knew that you just didn't last too long living on the streets. Some time someone would come along and cut my throat for a half-empty bottle and I would be in too much of a drunken stupor to stop them. Hell, most days I wish they would come and get it over with.

As I saw it, I had no future. I had no schooling other than high school, and a military school on how to mix ordnance. I could mix explosives with the best of them. They had taught me how to kill, and to stab someone and not even work at killing them. The only call for that line of work would be with the mob, and as disfigured as I was, I couldn't get close enough to anyone to harm them. Besides, I had promised God that day in the rice paddy that if he would let me live to get out of there, I would never kill anything again.

The wine was starting to warm me and I would drift off into a light sleep. Each time I awoke, I took a few more drinks and then would doze off again. I could hear the wind blowing harder and it was starting to get colder, as it was dark now. My heavy coat helped some, but I sure wished I was in the mission or over visiting Albeit at the hospital. I drank the rest of the first bottle of cheap wine and could taste the sour vinegar bile in my stomach. I knew I would be sick from the wine and not eating since morning. I tried to sleep but the chills and the shaking kept me from getting into a sound sleep. I lay there for hours in the dark, curled up as tight as I could get. I opened the other bottle and drank several long drinks. What did I ever do to deserve the kind of life I was living? Could you even call this living?

I had always been a fighter for what I wanted and believed in. Why had I given up? Did that she'll take my spirit, as well as half of my face? I still didn't want pity from anyone, but the way I looked, people couldn't look at me long enough to talk to me. I had tried several times to talk to people and I always got a bum's rush from them. I didn't even have the nerve to go see my mother. I just couldn't bear her to see me looking like this. The only clothes I had were what I was wearing. Bob over at the mission would try to keep clean clothes for some of us. The military surplus store gave him stuff, and the government sent out stuff for us, but it was a hassle to get anything from them. They always had to fill out a lot of paperwork and you had to see a doctor. Usually one that was a bigger drunk than we were. Some were dedicated veterans that truly wanted to help us. But mostly they spent too much time trying to tell us what we were doing wrong, instead of trying to really help us. I wasn't afraid to work. Hell, growing up on a farm milking cows and farming, that is all I knew how to do.

I don't how long I had been asleep or passed out maybe; something had awakened me. I could hear voices close by, in my drunken stupor. I just figured the cops were hassling me again.

"Come on out, you stinking bum," I heard someone call out. Then an object struck the side of the cardboard box I had been sleeping in. There wasn't much room up under the bridge structure, so I knew no one would come up in there. I pulled the box back and three young men stood there holding clubs.

"We're going to kick your ass, you homeless bastard."

I could tell they were as drunk as I was, and just trying to work up courage. Why they were after me I had no idea. The wine was wearing off and I was starting to get angry.

"You want a piece of me, sonny, come on in and get it," I said.

He poked at me with the stick, jabbing me in the stomach. I knew from my Ranger training what was coming next. On his next jab, I grabbed the stick and pulled hard toward me; this pulled the punk in close and I laid the wine bottle alongside of his head. I could tell by the way he went down that he wouldn't bother me for a little while, if at all this night. I had sobered up a lot and figured I might as well make a fight of it. Hell, it would get me warm anyway. I broke the bottom off the bottle and came out from under the bridge like my ass was on fire. The closest kid was a big guy maybe two hundred fifty pounds. One jab in the guts with the broken bottle let the air out of him, and he sobered up fast. I don't think he had ever seen that much blood before, not his own anyway. The third punk lost all interest in me and headed up the street on a dead run yelling like the devil was after him, and he was. I could still run pretty good and was hell bent on catching him, that's when I saw the police cruiser.

I gave up the chase and turned and ran up over the tracks for a swampy area by the expressway. I didn't slow down going through the water and came out by a fence that was too high to climb. As I crawled along the fence in the high weeds, I could hear police cars coming from every direction. I turned, got up, and went back into the water. It led me through a small culvert into the back of a construction company equipment yard. There was a large earthmover parked there. I crawled up into the back and lay there.

All the running and the wine, on an empty stomach, got to me and I started to throw up, I heaved there until I was exhausted. I knew the cops would never find me there, even if the three drunken kids told what they had done.

I was getting ready to leave when I heard the cops coming through the yard. I had forgotten about those damn dogs they use now, and the shepherd was hot on my trail. How he tracked me through all that water and the culvert, I don't know, and I still didn't think he could find me. I lay as quiet as I could. They milled around in the yard for a while and I was sure they could hear my heart beating. Then the damn dog started barking loud enough to wake the dead. I knew I was had at that time.

One officer said, "Show some hands or we will put gas in there." I stood up placing both hands on the side of the truck box. "Come on out," he said.

I climbed over the back and dropped to the ground. Then the bastard let that dog loose on me while I was lying face down on the ground. Lucky for me I still had on my heavy coat and that was all he grabbed. After I was cuffed, they stood me up, trying to blind me in the only eye I had with the damn flashlight.

"What are you doing in here?" he said.

"Trying to steal gas," was the only thing that came to mind, so that is what I told him. Hell, I was out of wine and needed something to drink.

"You smell like you fell in a damn wine barrel," he said. "What do you know about some young boys getting cut up over on Chesnut tonight?"

"Why would I know anything about that?" I asked.

"Where did you get all the blood on you from?"

I hadn't noticed but my right sleeve was covered with blood. "That dog chewed on my arm, and damn near tore it off. Why did you turn him loose on me after I was lying down?"

"He hadn't been fed tonight," he laughed. "Usually I find cleaner food for him, but tonight he needed a little roughage, he isn't shitting too good lately."

"You are under arrest for criminal trespassing and suspicion of assault. Anything you say will be used in court."

He read me all that crap about a lawyer being provided for me, and such. They placed me in the back of a patrol car and took me to the city jail. I asked for a lawyer. They asked which one I usually used.

"They're all the same, aren't they? You arrested me; you pick one that will make it easy for you."

I figured I was in deep shit anyway, so why cooperate with the bastard. He was a real ass. I never seem to get arrested by the good guys. I had only been arrested once before, and that was after I came home from Nam, and went to see my daughter. I punched out a smartass deputy sheriff that thought he was mister tough guy, and I had been thrown in the drunk tank several times. Most of those times they just turned us loose after we sobered up.

During the booking procedure they asked if I had ever been arrested before.

"Just for being drunk and being on the street late at night."

"How many times you been in the tank?"

"I would say, probably a half dozen times, I guess, give or take a couple."

About that time a cute little clerk came in with my record sheet and things started to change fast.

"Says here, Danny Boy, you've been locked up for assaulting a police officer."

"Yes, I did ninety days a couple years ago for slapping a county Mounty around that tried to get rough with me for no cause. It was a stupid thing to do. I had just come home from Nam and was on leave from the hospital. I went home to see my daughter, only the wife or ex-wife called the law on me. She said I was so horrible looking it would scare the kid. There was a little pushing match that started and soon fists were flying. I found out that it is pretty tough to whip three of them, and that damn mace is wicked stuff. I had faced tear gas while in basic, but it is nothing to what that mace does to you. It takes the fight out of you pretty quick."

My arm had started to hurt, and I thought maybe that damn dog did bite me after all. I stood up and took off my blood-stained coat and noticed I had a three-inch stab wound or cut on the inside of my right arm near the elbow. The wound was still seeping blood and I asked for a towel.

"Let's have a look at that," the officer said. "Hell, boy, that's no dog bite. You have been stabbed."

He got out a first-aid kit and put a gauze bandage on my arm. "Dan old boy, it looks like your assault just turned to self-defense, and with a little persuasion, I believe the criminal trespass can be dropped to a plea of self-preservation."

I really couldn't believe the turnaround of this officer's attitude; he started to seem halfway human. He said he would call the VA hospital and have an ambulance pick me up, but I would still have to go to court after my release and he would have the public defender contact me.

The ambulance was one of those military rigs that rode like a truck, but what the hell it was warm inside, and I would get a warm bed for the night, if I were lucky. The two medics looked at my arm and said about twenty stitches should be done. I waited in the emergency room for two hours before they would admit me. I didn't have any records or identification on me. I had left everything at the mission over a week ago when I changed clothes there. It took forever to look me up in the files. Then the stupid clerk said, "what are we here."

I said, "I don't know about you, but I have a stab wound to my arm that needs stitches."

He had to look at it too. Now that was twice it had been unbandaged, and he put another one on it, and then the damn paper work started. "Have you been here before, and what for?" and all that other crap.

I just said "No," to everything. If it showed I had been there for a drug problem he never reacted to it so I let it go. The doctor was a young-looking dude; much younger than me I thought. He had good manners and was very polite.

"How were you injured?" he asked.

I told him about the three boys and the fight and using the bottle to defend myself against the kid with the knife. I didn't remember ever seeing a knife, but if I could save my ass with a few little white lies so be it.

"Why did they attack you?" he asked.

"I think they were just out to harass someone and it was my bad luck to be in the wrong place at the wrong time."

He gave me a shot in the arm and put fourteen stitches in it.

"Do you want to be admitted?" he asked.

"Well, I wouldn't mind a warm bed, a bath and a hot meal or two."

"That's good, you could stand to dry out some. I will prescribe a sedative to help you sleep. Also, we have a specialist that I want to have a look at your eye. There is a new procedure now for dealing with burn scars. I think he can pretty you up some, and I don't think that eye is a total loss, if they can get some of the scar tissue out of the way. He won't be here for a couple of days, so you can either hang around, or come back and make an appointment with him."

"I will make an appointment. I don't like to stay around these places too long. I might need a drink. And that damn alcohol you guys' use is murder."

He grinned and rang for a nurse. "I'll see you in the morning," he said.

He left, and in about ten minutes a cute little nurse came in, picked up my file and said, "Follow me." We walked down a couple of halls to an elevator and went up several floors. She took me to a room that had two beds in it but both were empty.

She said, "The shower is in there," pointing to an adjoining room.

"There is also a gown on the shelf."

"Not one of those backless damn things, is it?"

She laughed and said, "I will see if I can find some pajamas for you."

I shut the door and soon she knocked and came in and handing me the pajamas, said she would be back later to tuck me in. I thought, baby, you can tuck me in anytime.

The shower was hot and I stood there for as long as I could without feeling guilty. There was a razor on the sink, so I decided to trim up a little. Man! I tell you I looked like hell! My face was scared, and whiskers growing in every direction; my hair was clear past my shoulders. My left eyelid was a burn scar, and was mostly closed over a white eye that I was totally blind in. My left ear was a mass of burned scars and only half there. I trimmed up my whiskers leaving a mustache and goatee.

Putting on the clean pajamas, I felt half like a human, and I think I was only half human. I had been living like an animal for three years. I had lost most all my body fat. I was skin and bones, and not much to look at. I was beginning to shake from the need of alcohol. I climbed into bed and rang for the nurse, and the meanest-looking woman I had seen in years appeared at my door and asked what I needed. I was afraid to tell her I needed a drink and afraid not to. I told her I had been on alcohol for three years and was going into shock from the need of it. I figured she would say "tough," but she said, "I have been there before, so we'll see what I can do for you."

Soon a doctor came in and said, "Are you having problems?"

"Yes, doc," I said, "I need a drink bad."

He looked at my chart and said, "I'll see what I can do."

The old nurse brought me some orange juice. "This has lots of sugar in it, so it will have to do."

Man, I thought, these people are crazy. I need a drink. I let the juice sit there for a long time but by now my stomach was having fits, so I sipped the orange juice. Hell, it was half vodka, they could have told me, but I guess that stuff is illegal to give to a patient.

After the juice, I felt relaxed and hungry, and I didn't want to bother anyone again, but soon the old nurse came back in. I asked her if I could get something to eat.

She said, "You want it here or would you like to go down to the cafeteria? I will get you a robe if you do."

"The cafeteria sounds good, if you will give me directions."

The cafeteria was in the basement and not many people were there. They stared at me a moment, when I came in, then went back to their conversations. I took a tray and got some meatloaf and all the trimmings. I even got a glass of milk, the first I had had in years, and I used to pull a lot of teats to get it. I was so full I didn't even have desert. My stomach had shrunk from not eating, so it didn't take much to fill me up. I went back to my room and really wanted a drink then. But I knew better than to push my luck. I crawled into bed and relaxed, and thought, this is what clean sheets feel like. I was just starting to get sleepy when that good-looking nurse came in.

She gave me a couple of pills to help me sleep. She then pulled the sheet up and tucked it around my shoulders. "I said I would tuck you in, didn't I?"

"Thank you," I said in a quiet embarrassed way. "You know you are the first woman that has been this close to me in over three years. I guess because of my looks, from my injury."

"You don't look so bad," she said, leaning over and kissing me on the cheek. She then gave me a long hug.

God, I never knew anything that simple could make you feel so good!

"I'll see you tomorrow," she smiled and walked out not looking back. That simple hug did a trip on me. Hell, I was a basket case. I almost broke out crying. The thoughts of Maty and our nights together, the warmness of her and the clean smell of her skin, just holding her to me and listening to her breath at night, these thoughts were really wrecking me.

I don't know when the sleeping pills kicked in, but I am glad they did or they would have had me in the physic ward by morning. The next thing I knew, it was morning and a lady came in and started cleaning up my room.

"So you're going home today?" she said.

"Yea, I guess so," I grunted. If she only knew! I had no home to go to, only the cold streets to welcome me. I got up and dressed. At least they had washed my clothes for me. I walked to the elevator, went down to the cafeteria and got coffee. I sat and sipped the coffee for a long time, finally getting a sweet roll to go with it. Afterwards, I just walked out of the building without checking out. It was cold on the street and I didn't know where to go, so I headed up toward town and the post office.

I had my check in the post office box that I shared with my brother. A whole two hundred and sixty-five dollars, also a note from Vick saying that Mom was near death, and that I really should go see her, that her vision was so bad she couldn't see what I looked like anymore, so I had nothing to worry about.

I was clean for a change and decided to go see her while I was still sober and didn't smell like a winery. I caught a bus that took me across town and dropped me off a couple blocks from the rest home. I hated doing this; what would I say? The lady at the desk really took a hard cold look at me when I walked in.

"May I help you?" she asked, looking down her nose at me like I had the damn plague or something.

"I came to see Mrs. Watts. I am her son."

"I thought she only had one son," the lady said in a snotty tone.

"Well, lady, she has two, and I am the one who got shot all to hell in Viet Nam trying to keep this wonderful country safe for people like you."

I guess it was fear or frustration or her attitude that set me off.

"Please follow me," she said, and walked off down the hall, stopping at a room with the door open. "She is in here, but I doubt if she is awake."

"That's ok," I said. "I won't wake her." I slipped into the room and looking at the frail old woman in the bed. I had to fight back the tears as I looked at her.

She moved and said, "Who is it?"

I leaned over and hugging her said, "It's me, Mom, Danny." I was surprised at the life this brought to her; she pulled me down onto her so hard I almost fell.

She said, "I thought the Army would let you come see me sooner than this."

"I was over in Viet Nam, Mom, that is a long ways from Springdale." I didn't know what else to say. She lay there with her eyes closed holding onto my hand. It was dark in the room, so I couldn't tell if she could see me, or just didn't want to look. Had Vick told her about my injury and the damage to my face? I didn't know and didn't care. I was finally there.

Soon, Mom was asleep. I sat there in the chair holding her hand for what seemed like hours. Finally, I put her hand back on her breast, got up and kissed her lightly, and walked out the door.

"When she wakes up, tell her that her son Danny was here, or she will just think she has been dreaming," I said to the lady at the desk. "Please come back and see her again," she said

It was dark out and the night was cold. I started walking toward Division Street and the mission. I needed a drink bad, and to somehow get my head straight. God, I couldn't believe that Mom looked so bad. Vick had said that losing the farm had killed Dad and done Mom in.

I was walking through a residential area and noticed a group of boys on the corner ahead of me. I turned and crossed the street and kept walking. Soon they were behind me, taunting me.

"Hey, are you a soldier boy," one hollered, "or just another street bum "We don't allow no street bums in this neighborhood."

Someone kicked me in the back. I turned around and got hit in the face. They were hitting and kicking me so fast I couldn't stop it. My mouth was split and I could taste blood. I knew I was in a lot of danger. As I went down, I just balled up and took the kicking and pounding. I could hear the sirens screaming, and figured finally the police were coming.

Next thing I knew, I was looking up at a blinding light, only I couldn't see it too good through my one eye. It was swollen mostly shut. Someone was asking, "Can you hear me? I tried to sit up, but the pain was more than I could bear. For a while, I thought I was back in a chopper in Nam. Only I couldn't hear any firing, just people talking, shaking me and asking questions. Then I remembered the boys and started to react. People were holding me and telling me I was all right, to relax, that I had been injured. I finally realized that I was in a hospital emergency room. My mouth was swollen and I was having trouble breathing through my nose. Blood was everywhere, and my hands were swollen and painful. I felt like I had been run over and was thinking I had been. I asked where I was and was told in the emergency room of the city hospital.

Again, they asked my name and I told them who I was, and to call the VA hospital for my medical records.

"Do you know what happened to you?" the doctor asked as he worked on me.

"Yea, I just got the hell beat out of me by a bunch of punks."

"You have a broken nose and one hand is broken. We are still checking for internal injuries. Is there someone we can call for you?" "Yea, the police," I said.

"They are waiting to talk to you, but I don't think you will be doing much talking for a few days. Do you have family we can notify? Or someone you live with?

"There is only me, doc, and I live on the street."

CHAPTER III

I graduated from Arco High in early June of 1965. Mary and I were married on the 4th of July that same year. The wedding was a small church service, and Artie was my best man.

When we saw Mary coming down the aisle, he leaned over and said, "You lucky bastard, you don't deserve her."

I smiled and said, "No, but I am going to get her."

We had a short honeymoon to Georgia to visit her aunt. Neither one of us had ever been with anyone else. So the wedding night was spent in a special way. Really getting to know each other. I can still smell her perfume, the smell of her hair and the warm, soft touch of her body. I had never loved anything or anyone so much. I held her so long that my arms ached. I never ever wanted to be away from her.

The visit with the aunt was a boring time for me, but I made the best of it for Mary's sake. The trip home was a quick drive, as I wanted to get home and help Dad on the farm. We had fixed up the little house real neat, with new furniture and I had put a new counter and cabinets in the kitchen. We had received lots of wedding gifts, so housekeeping was a snap for Mary. She would come out and ride the tractor with me all day long. We would stop and make love behind the hay bales that I would pile up. Dad was wise as to what was going on so he tried to never surprise us. We were almost caught by Sis one afternoon as she brought us out refreshments; lucky we heard the old pickup rattling over the rough ground. Time seemed to stand still for us in those days. I wanted them to go on forever.

It was in September that I got a letter from the draft board that my draft number was thirty-two. Saying that I would be called up to serve my country within ninety days. Mary was heartbroken and filled with fear. She would cry at night and became withdrawn from me at times. Dad had said if I told them I was married that I could probably get a deferment for a year or two or maybe permanent. I said yes and be just like my Uncle Bill and be called a damn draft dodger all my life. Dad had served in Korea and came back in one piece. Mary tried every way she could think of to get me deferred and could not understand why I didn't try harder to get out of going. It was in late November that I got my notice to report for a physical, and induction into the Army on December 5.

It was at this time Mary told me she was pregnant. For the first time I was filled with fear and didn't want to go. I held Mary close to me all night and listened to her sleep. I don't think I slept at all that night. Dad had grown silent and I could see the worry on his face. We had taken on more land to farm and signed a five-year lease on it. I knew he couldn't farm all that by himself, so I told him we would just have to hire someone to help, and with part of my military pay we could manage. After all, I would be gone for only two years. "A lot can happen in two years, son," he said.

I never thought so much could happen that would change my life forever.

Mom went about her daily chores as usual. I did notice that her hugs were tighter and longer than usual, and she seemed quieter. Sis had a new boyfriend that seemed to occupy all of her time. Artie had gotten a college deferment and tried to get me to apply to a college and see if I could get out of going. I told him I would go and get it over with, that he would have to go when he got out of college anyway. He said, not if I can help it.

December the 5th finally arrived and everyone took me to the bus. Mary had cried all night and was sick with morning sickness. She looked real pale, and had lost weight from the morning sickness and worried about me leaving. Everyone was crying, even Dad, though he tried to hide it. Artie told me not to worry that he would help Dad and keep an eye on Mary and see that everything worked out all right.

I arrived at the Army recruit induction center in Texas on the evening of the 6th. We were fed and bedded down for the night. There were about fifty worried and sad young men there just like me. I couldn't sleep that night for worrying about Mary and my folks. I knew this was going to be a hard two years on everyone. I had never thought of being drafted even after I registered on my eighteenth birthday. I hadn't paid much attention to the war in Viet Nam. I had watched some of the protesters at the colleges on television and I disapproved of what they were doing, but never gave much thought to the men in the service. Several of the guys in my class had joined the Marines and Navy after graduation.

I lay there listening to the sounds in the night. I could hear the noise of the heating system fans cut on and off. I could hear people crying and hear men getting up and going to the bathroom, the sound of a passing car now and then. I wondered what lay ahead of me for the coming day. I must have dozed off for it only seemed like a few minutes and all the lights came on and people were hollering and kicking the bunks we slept in. We were made to strip the mattress covers off the bunks and put the mattress over the top bunk and stand at attention at the end of our bunks.

We were marched to a mess hall where we were served what I thought was a pretty good breakfast. I made a comment about the food to one of the guys. He said, "Wait until you eat those MRE's, then see how good you like Army food." We were then marched to what looked like a large gymnasium. We were given a stack of papers to fill out dealing with any sickness, disease, or ailments we had. We were than told to strip to our under shorts. When our names were called, we were sent to another room and examined by a military doctor. Then shuffled over to another room to a dental chair. After our teeth had been checked, we were allowed to dress again and then called to attention. Told to raise our hands and then we were sworn into the United States Army.

We were given a large envelope and told to put all personal papers and jewelry except wedding bands into it; all pictures, credit cards and any money over twenty dollars. We were told that this would be returned on completion of basic training. We were then measured somewhat for clothing. They gave each of us a large duffel bag and as we walked through a line of bins, military clothing was stuffed into it. We were then marched to a barracks and told that this would be our home for the next ten weeks.

A big black sergeant said in not too kind words: "From now on I will be your mother and father, anything you need must come through me. It is my job to make soldiers out of you. Keep your mouth shut and don't talk unless you are talked to by me."

After instructions on how to fold our clothes, we were required to stencil our name and service number on all our clothes. Then we got to hand wash everything, run it through a dryer, and then told to strip and put on military clothing.

We were then assigned a bunk and a foot locker and shown how to store our gear. Then we were paraded outside and told to line up. We were put in a line according to our height, and told to learn this position, and this was where we were to line up each time we fell out. Whatever that meant! The sergeant then, with the aid of some corporal that didn't look old. enough to shave, let alone be in the Army, showed us how to march and do close order drills. They marched us back to the gymnasium; it was known as the drill hall. They had us strip off our shirts and march single file down a line of people on each side of us, and we must have been given at least five shots, for God only knows what.

Each day was filled with more of the same. We ran everywhere we went. Had physical fitness drills that were a lot like football practice, only longer and harder.

Time went by pretty fast and I had no real problems. After the second week we got mail. I had a letter from Mary for each day I had been gone, and she had put her perfume on them. Man, this made me so damn horny I couldn't stand smelling them. After the third week we were allowed one, twenty-minute phone call twice a week. I lived for these nights when I could talk to Mary and the folks. Mom and Dad would always say Hi, and then leave Mary alone to talk to me. I wanted her so bad. She had begun to get over the morning sickness some. She said the doctor told her everything was fine, and she would have a good healthy baby. I looked forward to the daily letters. My brother Vick was home from college and was helping Dad for a while; he would add a note on the bottom of Mom's letters. Sis would write to me once or twice a week telling me everything that was going on, at school and in town.

Time went by quickly, each day was the same boring routine. It wasn't long until we had only two weeks left to go before graduation from basic. We were putting in for what schools and places we wanted to be stationed. I asked for Ranger school, mainly because it was in Oklahoma and I wanted to be close to home. The drill sergeant told me I was nuts and that the Ranger program was one of the toughest in the Army. I was in great shape and figured I could take anything they threw at me. I really didn't care as long as I could be close to Mary.

Graduation day came with all the parade and fanfare that comes with it. Mom, Dad and Mary were there. I was proud to show her off to some of the buddies I had. I drew the Ranger school in Fort Sill, Oklahoma. I also had fourteen days leave, so we drove straight home. That first night home with Mary was out of this world. She had started to show a little, so things were done with care.

We went out with Artie and his girl to a movie and dinner. Artie seemed awfully quiet. He kept looking at Mary.

I said, "What has college done to you? Seems like it has taken some of the fire out of you old buddy." He just smiled and said he was tired.

I tried to get as much done at the farm as I could while I was home. Dad and I got all the buildings cleaned out, and the hay equipment ready for haying. I spent two days plowing for Dad, with Mary riding on the tractor with me. I didn't think it was such a good idea, but she seemed ok by it all. Only too quickly it was time for me to report to Fort Sill. Vick volunteered to drive there. Mary and I rode in the back and talked most of the way. She was pretty sad but kept her composure. I checked in at the base headquarters. Saying goodbye to Mary was hard, but I assured her I would come home on a weekend as soon as I could.

Ranger school wasn't at all what I had expected. We were checked out on every kind of weapon that the military had. Most of the time we spent running and doing muscle-building exercises, watching films, and going to school on military tactics. We learned to repel out of helicopters, over cliffs, and scale walls. Doing all this with a sixty-pound pack on our back and carrying weapons of all types.

We had three weeks of emergency first-aid training on how to control bleeding, treat victims for shock, and how to pick up and carry a wounded person for a long distance. It was a grueling task. The forty-mile marches with a full pack and no sleep were the worst. After five weeks I got a three-day pass. Mary had driven down to get me, against my wishes, but I was happy she was there. We called Mom and Dad and decided to just stay there. There were a lot of things I wanted to show Mary, both on and off the base. The three days went by swiftly and I had to get back on base. We rented a place for Mary to stay the week, and I conned my instructor to let me off base every other night. These times spent with her were the most precious hours of my life. Mary came down and spent several weekends with me. Soon it was graduation time for the Ranger group I was in. Dad was having some health problems, so Mary and brother Vick and his girlfriend were the only ones from my family to attend.

I only had two days off and Mary and I spent those together, just holding onto and loving each other. I had never felt depression before, and it is a very sick feeling. I tried not to show that I was worried or depressed. Monday came and I left Mary crying at the front gate, not knowing when I would see her again. We were told to pack our gear and be ready to move out in a day's notice. We were going to the Philippines to further our training. We left Oklahoma and flew to San Francisco. We had a two-hour layover there. I tried to call Mary from the airport, but no one was home. I slept sitting up in the airport lounge, until we were told to board. The flight to Hawaii was a long, quiet ride. We arrived about midday to a warm pretty place on Oahu. We were to be here for two days of orientation. I called Mary that night and talked until I ran out of money. She hung up crying; this depressed me even more.

After the orientation in Hawaii, we loaded up in the middle of the night and flew to Luzon, Philippines. We were all dog tired and hungry. Upon our arrival we were assigned a barracks, given time to stow our gear, and told to fall out and assemble in four lines. We were assigned to a company and divided up into squads of twelve men each. We were than assigned to a group of four men. In my group were Larry Morgan, Bill Thomas and Doc Carson. Doc was our medic; he was from York, Pennsylvania. His dad was some high-powered attorney. Doc had flunked out of med school and decided to try the Army before going back, much to his father's dislike. Larry was from Russell, Kansas, and a farmer like myself. Bill was from Brownsville, Texas, and had grown up around the oil fields and seemed to be a pretty rough cookie.

Doc and I became friends immediately; we both seemed to have the same outlook on life. The training in the Philippines was hot and miserable. We trained all day and night. We were too tired to eat and too hot to sleep. I hadn't heard from Mary in several weeks, as our mail hadn't caught up with us. We finally got paid and I was able to call home. Mary really seemed depressed. She said she was thinking of moving up to Springdale and staying with her sister, until after the baby was born. This was when I told her I was being sent to Viet Nam. She started crying and couldn't seem to stop. I tried to tell her how much I loved her and that I would write every day.

I still hadn't heard from her, but we were supposed to get mail that week. When the mail did arrive I had about twenty letters and didn't know which one to open first. Reading them filled me with excitement and depression. The baby was starting to move and Mary had found out we were going to have a girl. She was going through a name book to try and pick a name that would fit. God, how I wanted to be with her to just hold her, to smell her, and touch her. She still put her perfume on the letters; smelling this and thinking of loving her just drove me up the wall.

It was one hot morning in March that we were told to pack up and be ready to travel in 45 minutes. We were on our way to Viet Nam. The flight to Nam was a long, hot, miserable ride. A lot of men were airsick, or maybe like myself sick with fear; we were headed to a combat zone where anything could happen. We landed at a place called Long Binh. There were a lot of troops there that made some pretty crude remarks as we unloaded our gear. I found out later that they were on their way home on the same plane that had brought us in.

We were fed at a field kitchen. The food wasn't too bad, but about half warm and I have no idea what it was, but I was hungry so I ate it and drank the tea. We were able to take a shower there but had to put on the same clothes as our gear was stored ready to be sent to Da Nang, our next duty station. We slept that night on a cot set up in a large tent; we were given one blanket, which I didn't think I would need. I found out, however, it can get pretty chilly early in the morning. The next day we were loaded into helicopters and had a long ride to Da Nang. Some of the country didn't look too bad and a lot was like a jungle. Doc Carson and I sat and tried to talk above the roar of the chopper engines. We both had a lot of concern about what was happening to us, and what was going to happen. We have seen a lot of combat films and been given orientation on what to expect. I had hunted rabbits and quail on our farm and seen a deer once but didn't have the heart to shoot it. I wondered if I could shoot someone that was shooting at me and decided I could, if it came to that.

When we arrived at Da Nang we were marched to a dug-out living area, that was covered with wood and sheet metal, and sand bags all around it and on the roof.

"This is home, boys, get used to it," the corporal said.

The four of us in our squad were assigned bunks and told where the showers and latrines were. The shower felt great, but we had to put the same dirty clothes that we had been wearing back on, as our gear hadn't arrived yet.

We were called to fall out for muster, and given a welcome speech, by some bird colonel, after which myself and several other men were told to report to headquarters. There we met Sergeant James and Corporal Allen. We were given instructions on standing guard at one of the listening posts outside the base. Larry Morgan and I were assigned to post three, which was about two hundred yards north and outside the fenced-in area. Corporal Allen took us out after dark, which I didn't like. I am not afraid of the dark, but things that I can't see, that move around in the dark, scare the hell out of me.

The listening post was a hole about four-foot deep, and about four-foot square, with logs and sand bags piled around it. One of us was to stay awake at all times and report any suspicious activity. There was a phone hooked up there and we were given fifty rounds of ammo and two grenades each. We also were given a flare pistol and six flares and told to shoot a flare to light up anything we saw moving outside the area. We were ordered to lock and load our weapons and to put the grenades at the ready. If we saw anyone out there, we were to call headquarters, shoot the flare and open fire. This was a restricted area and no one was to be there after dark. The corporal then moved on down the line to the next post with some other men.

I had spent many nights on the farm sitting in a dark barn waiting for a cow to calve, or little pigs to be born. I loved sitting alone on the riverbank at night cat fishing and listening to the frogs along the river. But this was different. I told Morgan to go ahead and sleep, that I would take the first watch.

"Hell, man," he said, "I couldn't sleep now if I took a whole box of sleeping pills."

"Yea, I know what you mean."

We sat and listened to the sounds of the night. It wasn't long until the noise at the base quieted down. Then the sounds of the night started. I could hear the bawling of a water buffalo off in the distance. We waited there for several minutes both too scared to talk, feeling that neither of us knew just what we were doing out there. I could hear sounds made by what I figured were frogs or insects. Did Nam even have frogs or singing bugs?

I didn't know, but I can tell you I thought this: *tomorrow if I am alive I am damn sure going to find out, I don't care how stupid I sound; I intend to get some answers front the older men.* Anyone that had been in this country more than a week, I planned to ask a lot of questions. This was one man that planned to survive this damn war. Morgan finally drifted off to sleep. He tried to talk some even as he was dozing off. I sat there listening to his heavy breathing and got to thinking about Mary; how I would hold her and listen to her breathe. I pulled one of her last letters out of my pocket and sat and sniffed her perfume.

It was almost time for the baby to be born, and she had moved in with her sister in order to be closer to the hospital. I hadn't received any letters in several weeks, so I just read the old ones over again. Our mail and lost gear should be found soon. I don't know how long I had been sitting there thinking of her.

Suddenly, the sky was white with a blinding light that lit up the whole area. I could hear yelling then the pop, pop, pop sound of a M-16. Then came the explosion of a grenade, then another. I kicked the safety off on my rifle and then dropped the damn thing.

I was so damn scared that I couldn't swallow. Morgan jumped half out of the pit, clawing for a grenade, and his rifle at the same time.

"What in the hell is going on?" he cried.

"Beats the shit out of me. Call headquarters and see what we are to do." We rang and rang but the line was busy. I guess every post along the line was trying to call in. By now the flare had gone out and it was darker than I had ever seen it before. It was so quiet you could hear a gnat fart a mile away. We both sat there in total silence for a long time, then the light on the phone lit up. I picked it up and said, "Post three."

"You boys all right out there?" the voice on the other end said.

"I said, "Yes, sir, what happened?"

"One of the new guys thought he heard something and pulled the panic button, but don't let it worry you. Keep your eyes and ears open. You can never tell when these little bastards will try and sneak up close enough to throw a satchel charge on you."

"Thanks a lot, sir," I said. "I feel a whole lot better."

I told Morgan I didn't think my heart could take many more nights like this.

He said, "I don't know about you, but I am still shaking. Why would they put two green men out in a place like this?" "Beats me!" I said.

Morning finally came. I was still shaking. I didn't know if it was from the tension, fear or cold. We had breakfast in a huge tent that was set up for a mess hall. The food was hot and filling. I wanted a few hours of sleep, and headed for the houch, as our sleeping area was called. But first I wanted to know what kind of critters prowled the night in this place.

I went into headquarters and looked up Sergeant James. I asked about animals and other things that made a sound in the night. Before he could answer, a couple of old timers started talking about snakes, huge rats and mean monkeys.

Sarge said, "Don't pay any attention to those two. What you are listening for are people sounds, the rattling of metal, footsteps, the clanking of ammo boxes or digging noises, the snapping of a twig. Now go get some rest; at sundown we are going out on patrol and try and set up an ambush on their trail."

I took time to write a short letter to Mary. I hadn't heard from her in over four weeks, even though we did get some mail in. I wasn't too concerned as the baby was past due, and for all I knew I could have been a father already.

I awoke about four in the afternoon covered with sweat and hungry. Morgan and Thomas were sitting at a table cleaning weapons, and Doc was over at the medical tent picking up supplies for tonight's patrol. I grabbed my towel and headed for the showers; after a quick shower, we headed for the mess tent. Chow was good and we had cold milk for a change.

We checked our weapons and loaded up with ammo and grenades and fell out and waited for Sarge outside the briefing room. There were fourteen of us, counting Sarge and Corporal Allen. We also grabbed three packs of MRE's, which are packed, dehydrated food. We filled our canteens and I stuffed two more water bottles in my pack. We rubbed on insect repellent, and camoed our face and hands. Corporal Allan and I took point. I sure hoped he knew where he was going, for I sure was lost. We marched in single file for about two hours then came to a small village of thatch houses and animal pens made from poles and bamboo. We skirted the village and started up over a hill. About halfway up we hit a trail that was about six feet wide and grown over on top by vines and trees.

Two of the new guys set up trip wire mines across the trail and we set up detonation charges on each side, about a hundred yards from where the trip wires were, on each end. We each picked a spot where we could see the trail and were told to keep quiet and not to move around. That if a flare was shot up and we heard fire, to give them everything we had. God I was scared, and shaking so hard my teeth were chattering like I was cold; but all the time I was soaked in sweat.

HOMELESS

We had been there about four hours, and I must have fallen asleep, but I don't know how, when the whole sky lit up. There were people everywhere. The trip wire mine blew and everyone started screaming and firing; people in black pajama-like clothes were pushing carts, bicycles and carrying big loads. Two of them ran right at me. I just pulled the trigger and kept pulling it. I threw both my grenades but don't remember pulling the pins. Things were exploding everywhere! Then the detonation charges were set off and the whole world shook. We were receiving heavy fire from down the trail and I could hear the whine of the bullets all around me.

My ammo was almost gone and I wasn't sure where the cans of extra ammo were and I was afraid to move. There were men screaming for medics, and it seemed that Doc was everywhere at once. Then all was quiet. Someone touched me on the shoulder and I jumped half out of my trench.

"You all right?" Sarge asked.

"I think so," I said.

"You done all right, boy. We got a couple boys hurt, but not bad. I think they were hit by our own explosions. We are going to sit tight until first light, so be alert. Get some more ammo when it comes by, and Watts, next time you throw a grenade, pull the pin. They make more noise that way. Scares hell out of the VC too." With that he rubbed his hand through my hair and was gone.

CHAPTER IV

Daytime was a long time coming. I could hear people moving and people moaning. I was afraid to shoot and wished someone would shoot up a flare again. It got all too quiet all of a sudden. I listened so hard, my ears hurt. It was like I was the only one out there; afraid to move, I just tried to dig deeper into the small impression I was in.

Suddenly, all hell broke loose. There was heavy fire coming from down the trail, and mortars were going off all around me. I emptied the M-16 several times in the direction the fire was coming from. Then large shells started exploding all around where the small arms fire was coming from. I could hear people yelling, but it was another language. I wished I had some grenades. The heavy shelling kept up for about fifteen minutes, but it seemed like it would never stop. Then things were quiet. Suddenly, someone touched me again. It was Sarge!

"Damn it, Sarge! Make some noise, don't slip up on me that way." "Yea! And get my butt shot off by you," he said. "Welcome to combat, soldier! You have just earned your first combat citation and medal. Don't go trying for a damn Purple Heart now. We already have three wounded and I don't need any more casualties."

With this said he moved on. It was starting to get light enough I could see the trail, and what looked like a damn bus wreck. There was stuff blown all over the place and I thought I could see people lying in the ditches and the trail itself.

For the first time reality set in, and I realized what had happened to me. I had been in combat and had killed the enemy, or at least shot at him. It got light quick and Corporal Allen and I moved down to where the shooting had been coming from. The large shells had hit home, and there were dead bodies all around. I got sick. Man! This could have been us! Corporal Allen said to do a quick body count and get the hell out of there. Then he shot! I jumped and hit the ground with the safety off. He was standing over a black-clad body.

"Wasn't dead," he said, as casual as shooting a rabbit. We counted twenty-three bodies or parts. There were nine more killed on the trail. We picked up all the ammo they had left, and one of my unexploded grenades. We never did find the other one.

"Lucky that you didn't get it back in your face, son," the sergeant said.

Thomas had been hit in the chest and was in bad shape. Two other men had wounds to the face and arms from shrapnel. We called in a chopper for the wounded and carried them to a small clearing. Two choppers showed up. Doc Morgan and I went with the three wounded men and the rest of the squad left in the other chopper. At least they didn't make us walk home. After we were in the air I started to shake and couldn't stop. Doc tried to talk to me, but I just wasn't hearing him. After we landed and got the wounded unloaded, Doc said for me to go to the infirmary and he would meet me there. By the time he got there I had settled down some, and after a straight shot of booze from Doc I was ok. They flew Thomas out that evening and I never heard about him again.

We were called to a debriefing meeting that evening with all the brass. Each of us had to write down what we observed, how much ammo we thought we used and how many kills we thought we made, if any. We were congratulated for a job well done, and told we were to receive a battle citation plus the Viet Nam medal.

After chow, which I didn't eat much of, and a shower, I tried to sack out, but sleep wouldn't come. Why had we killed these people? They weren't shooting at us! I guess we got to them first, was all I could figure out. Search and destroy were our orders.

We were assigned to guard the base for the next couple of weeks. Every day and night, patrols were going out and men were getting killed and wounded. I had been in this country for two months now. I finally got a letter from Mary and a picture of a newborn baby girl. I was a father! She hadn't named the baby yet. The letter was short as she said she was tired and would write more later.

I stuck the picture of my daughter on the wall above my bunk. I was congratulated by all the guys, and they called me Pappy for a few days.

The next day we were formed into two squads and told we would be flown close to the Laosian border and would be in the field for a couple of weeks. It had started to pour rain every afternoon and then it would clear off and get steamy hot. There were four chopper loads of us, and we were set down on a small cleared-out area in the bush. Other troops were already there. They had made a makeshift base of sorts, dug a lot of rifle pits and sandbagged the area. Also, there were mined areas that were marked, going out, but coming in you better follow the wire that led you in.

This was a pretty quiet area for the first week. Then we started going on patrol and would stay out several days at a time. There seemed to be little leeches everywhere. We used tons of insect repellent, but they still got on you. At night they would get around your eyes and, in your nose, and mouth if they could. You would bleed like hell after you pulled them off. We kept our pant legs tucked in and our collars buttoned tight, as they would get into any body orifice they could.

We were supplied in the field by a supply drop from a chopper, even got mail. I had a letter from my brother Vick, but nothing from Mary. This upset me a lot, as I hadn't heard from her since I got word of the baby being born. Vick said he had some bad news to tell me, and I choked with fear, as to what I was about to read. Dad has had a heart attack and is in the hospital, they don't know how much damage he has to his heart as yet, but it doesn't look good. Also I went by to check on Mary and the baby. Her sister said she moved out and she didn knew where she had moved to. She has a stack of letters from you, that she hasn't picked up for weeks.

My stomach started to churn. I was getting sick, my throat tightened up and I wanted to leave. I walked off into the bush and cried and fought back the urge to kill something, myself or anyone around me. God, this couldn't be happening. I loved her more than life itself and I know she loved me. I never felt so helpless as I did at that moment.

Doc had come looking for me; somehow, he could read all of us and could tell when something wasn't right. I heard him call my name. "Watts, old buddy, is something wrong?" he asked. I handed him the letter and stood there shaking as he read it.

"I wish I could get you a trip home, but there is no way out of here short of getting killed or wounded," he said. "I doubt if things are as bad as it sounds. Take a deep breath and shake it off. It is things like this that gets your ass shot off out here."

"I flat don't give a damn," I said. "These little VC bastards better look out now, for I am going to be one killing son of a bitch."

I couldn't eat that night and slept very little. We could hear small arms fire several times during the night and knew some of the patrols had run into trouble. They would come back in at first light carrying their dead and wounded. A chopper would come in, pick up the wounded and leave a new replacement. The dead would be put into body bags and picked up later.

Our turn came for patrol. We moved out about two in the afternoon. I volunteered for point man. No one but Doc could understand why. We were scarcely a mile from the camp when we were hit by a force a lot bigger than us.

One minute, things were quiet and the next there were explosions, gunfire, and men yelling everywhere. Sarge was calling for support. I was firing as quick as I could load and squeeze the trigger. There were men down on both sides of me and bleeding badly. I tried to put a pressure bandage on a leg wound and fire at the same time. Doc and the other medic were exposing themselves to enemy fire, carrying men and dragging men to shelter. I tried to keep an eye on Doc and see where the heaviest fire was coming from.

Soon planes were screaming in and fire was everywhere. I had never seen or felt so many explosions. Wounded men were screaming in agony. Doc didn't have enough morphine for everyone. Sarge called for an evacuation chopper, and a medic lift. Soon choppers were coming and going in a steady stream from the little clearing behind us. I looked up just in time to see Doc Carson go down. He tried to get up and fell back. I ran to him and pulled him into a trench. Both our medics were wounded so I tried to stop the bleeding on Doc's head wound.

Most of the shooting had stopped for the exception of a little small arms fire, which was coming from the left of us. I dragged Doc toward a chopper and was almost there, when an explosion went off in my face. I couldn't hear or see, I could feel myself falling and knew I was down. Someone grabbed me and drug me to the medivac chopper. I was safely aboard and could see a little. Then I could see Doc, lying out there. I jumped out and ran for him. He was covered in blood. I picked him up and started for the chopper. One leg went out from under me, and I knew I had been hit. The door gunner was raking fire back and forth over us and yelling at me all the time to get aboard! I crawled toward the chopper dragging Doc with me. The chopper started to move; and the door gunner jumped out and grabbed Doc and threw him aboard. I managed to crawl in just as it lifted off.

I knew I had been hit but didn't know how bad. I could hear the ringing in my ear and the skin hung down over my left eye. I could see a little and knew someone was wrapping my head in a bandage. I tried to move, but my leg wouldn't work right. I was told to hang on, that we would be at the field hospital in a couple minutes. Then the pain hit me. It felt like the whole side of my face was on fire. My left leg felt like someone was stomping on it. I could hear myself screaming, as I tried to sit up. Through blurred vision out of one eye, I could see Doc lying there covered in blood and not moving. There were wounded men all over the floor of the chopper, and other men sitting holding onto bandaged and bloody people.

I prayed to God to get me out of this. Only a few days earlier I had thought about taking my own life, now I was praying to live, and for Doc to live. Dear God let me live through this and I will never kill anything or anyone again.

I made promises that I probably wouldn't keep. I was screaming with pain, as were other men. The floor of the chopper was covered in blood. It trickled out the door and blew back onto the skids and windows. We finally touched down and they lifted us out and placed us on the ground. There seemed to be doctors and nurses everywhere. They took Doc, first; he was covered in blood and I couldn't see how he could still be alive. I started to access my own injuries. I knew that the bones in my leg were shattered. I could feel them move when I tried to lift it. I couldn't see out of my left eye and had blurred vision in the other one. My ear and the side of my face felt like mush. They had given me a shot upon arrival and most of the pain was gone.

All I could remember was a blinding flash; I couldn't figure out what had hit me. As I lay there on the ground, I tried to piece together what had happened, and who was wounded. Everything went black. The next thing I remember was waking up and my whole face was bandaged. Both eyes were covered, and there was a cast of sorts on my leg. I was lying in a bed with clean sheets. I could hear people moaning and talking. I lay there worrying about how bad I was hurt. The sound of a woman's voice brought me out of my trance. "Are you in any pain?" she asked.

She was holding my wrist. I supposed she was checking my pulse.

"Yea," I said. "My face feels like it is on fire, and my leg is throbbing."

"You have a pretty bad burn on your face and your leg was broken. The leg will be all right, but the burns will need a lot of special treatment. You will be flown to a burn center in Okinawa, Japan. We are giving you a sedative to help you sleep."

I asked about Doc Carson; I couldn't remember his name. She said she would check the charts and see if a medic named Carson was there.

The next time I awoke they were moving me out to the ambulance.

Myself and several other wounded soldiers were loaded into a plane on stretchers and strapped in, then we were air born. Several nurses were asking questions and talking to us. I kept asking what was happening to me. I must have slept for hours as the next thing I remember I was being carried down a ramp and placed in what I believed to be another ambulance.

After a short ride, I was placed on a gurney and wheeled into a building. They put me in a bed and asked if I needed anything. I was still about half goofy from the pain killer so I said, "Yes, get me something to read." There was total silence. Then someone said, "He will be ok!" I was left alone to listen to the sounds around me and to try to figure out what was going on.

There were other people in the room. I could hear soft talking and an occasional cough. I could hear people moan and beds squeak, hear people walking around and things clinking and things rolling. I could even smell food, though I wasn't hungry. I tried to remember when I had eaten last, or when I last went to the restroom. Everything seemed a blank.

Finally, someone came in and touched me. He said he was Doctor somebody, I couldn't understand his name. He spoke with an accent, he may have been Japanese. Hell, I didn't care, all I wanted was to quit hurting and to be able to see.

"We are going to take you into surgery and have a look at your face," he said.

The next thing I remembered was waking up in a room with curtains all around my bed. My head was bandaged but my right eye was left uncovered so I could see. My vision was still blurred, and I felt sick to my stomach. I finally decided that was hunger. I was as dry as a popcorn fart. I would have drank anything. I can't remember ever being that thirsty.

I lay there for what seemed forever. Finally, a nurse stuck her head in and said, "So you are finally awake." "May I have some water?" I asked.

"Not just yet," she said. "I will get you a glass of crushed ice; that will help some."

I thought I would die of thirst before she ever returned.

"How are you feeling?" she asked.

"Thirsty," I said. "My face hurts like hell and my leg has felt better. "

"Good!" she said. "That way we know you don't have too much nerve damage."

The ice tasted great.

"The doctor will be by to see you in a little while." Then she left. I drifted off to sleep, for how long, I have no idea. The doctor awakened me when he came in. He was an older, Oriental man that spoke with a broken accent.

"You were hurt pretty bad," he said. "You have a badly burned ear and your left eye is scarred. We won't know how badly until it heals some more. What hit you?"

"I have no idea. It could have been a phosphorous round. The VC use them a lot instead of tracers. All I can remember is a blinding white explosion. Hell, I was safe in the chopper and Carson was down and I couldn't leave him. Is it possible to find out how he is?" "Who is Carson?" he asked.

"He was my best friend and our medic. He got hit in the face and was bleeding bad when they took him off the chopper."

"We will see what we can find out."

That was the last time I tried to find out about him. I was still in Okinawa when I got word that my father had suffered a fatal heart attack the day before I was wounded. It took some time to locate me. Most of our patrol was wiped out. And none of the new guys knew me. Sergeant James was wounded but survived, I found out later.

I still hadn't gotten any word from Mary. I tried to call her sister, but she had changed phone numbers or moved. I got sick every time I thought of her. I had lost everything when I left Nam. All I had was my hospital clothes. How was I going to get her back? How long was I going to be here? How bad was I going to look? I guess most of my hair was burned off. Would it ever come back? I had too many questions and too much time to think about them.

They took my bandages off one day and I asked to see and was refused. I had surgery on my ear and eyelid and was sedated for a couple of days. When I was able to go in a wheel chair, they told me I was going to be flown to the states, to some hospital in Baltimore, Maryland.

It was a long flight and I slept as much as I could. I talked to some other guys that had been burned pretty badly. We were all headed to the same place. Our nurse was a pretty blond girl from Texas and she did everything she could to cheer us up. Every time I looked at her, all I could do was think of Mary. Why hadn't I heard from her? Was she sick? There were so many questions that I had, that I didn't have answers to. The hospital in Maryland was a huge place. I was placed in a ward with about six other guys. They kept coming and going. I never got to know anyone long enough to learn anything about them.

I had been here about five weeks, and the bandages had been removed. For the first time I got a look at myself. I was in shock at what I saw. My left ear was burned half off and was a swollen mass of flesh. I was burned badly all over that side of my face and my left eye was still bandaged.

Most of the hair on the left side was gone, just a big, burned, purple and red scar. The doctor said not to worry that a skin graft could fix most of it. I had regained some hearing in that ear, and my other eye was fine; so guess I had something to be thankful for.

My brother Vick showed up one morning. I was so glad to see him I could have jumped out of bed, but I still had the cast on. We visited for awhile and then I asked if he had any news about Mary. He just sat there and stared out the window.

"What is it?" I asked.

"It isn't good, Dan. I hate to tell you this! She has moved in with your buddy Artie and filed for divorce."

The most sickening feeling hit me like a bomb. I couldn't breathe and I couldn't talk. I wanted to scream. God only knows how this hurt.

"Why? Why would they do me this way? I knew Artie had always had an eye for her, but I would never have thought he would ever do this to me. What about the baby?" I asked.

"Mom is the only one in the family that has seen her. She said she looks a lot like you." Vick got up and walked out of the room.

A nurse came in and added something to the IV drip that was going into me. Next thing I knew the room was dark and quiet and Vick was gone.

I lay there and cried in the dark. I asked God to take me from this place and remove all this hurt and pain. A chaplin came into my room that morning and asked me a lot of questions about Mary and my little girl. Hell, she was almost a year old and I didn't even know what her name was.

He asked me a lot of questions about what I would do when I was discharged. I told him I didn't know. That my father had died while I was in Nam, and the bank had repossessed the farm. I had gotten word, through my brother, that my wife had moved in with my best friend and filed for divorce.

"Seems like you have been given a heavy load all at once," he said.

"Sir! Why, if there is a God, would he do this to me?"

"I don't have that answer," he said, "We must remain strong and keep the faith."

"I believe I lost that when I lost Mary, sir!" I said. "A man must have a reason to live, and someone to live for, even if it is just himself. This damn war has taken everything from me! My wife, my pride, and my face. Just what do I have left to live for?"

"Your daughter," he said. With that he got up, placed his hand on mine, and said, "Don't ever give up on the Lord, son. I will be in to see you tomorrow." Then he handed me a bible and said, "All the answers are with God." Then he left.

I lay there for a long time, denying God, and feeling sorry for myself one minute and getting mad enough to kill the next. I loved Mary so much. She was my wife. How could she turn to someone else? Especially Artie.

Sleep wouldn't come that night. I just lay there and ran my whole life through my mind. Why didn't I try and get out of going to the Army? I could still have Mary, and Dad would still be here. I would have made the farm work and taken all the stress off him. Here I was disfigured and didn't even know if I would walk on two good legs again. I drifted off to sleep wondering what would come of my life.

Days drifted by slowly and then turned to weeks. I got a few letters from Mom and Vick. Sis wrote when she could; she was in college. Mary had moved, and no one seemed to know where. I still didn't know my daughter's name and she was over a year old.

They finally took the cast off my leg. It looked bad; it was all shriveled up and crooked. I couldn't straighten it. The doctor said it would fill out with use, that all the muscle had deteriorated and with therapy it would eventually be almost as good as new. It was that word "almost" that worried me. I worked hard exercising it. The hospital had a weight room and a hot bath. I lifted weights and tried to work out as much as I could.

I finally got a look at my eye. It had a scar across it and was white. I could tell light from dark and that was all. I accepted the fact that I was going to be blind in that eye. I could walk with crutches now, and even a few steps without them. The hours in the weight room were putting muscle back where I used to have it.

I was sleeping better now, and they were trying to wean me off the pills. I still woke up at night thinking of Mary, wanting her in the worst way. I needed someone to love, to hold and to hold me. I could get a hug out of some of the nurses, but it only made the wanting in me that much worse. I asked the doctor when I could get out of there and he said as soon as I could run a block. The Army had given me a medical discharge and a small disability pension of four hundred and eighty-four dollars. How was I going to live on that?

It finally came: the day that I could leave the hospital. I was transferred to a veteran's hospital in Springdale. I rode a bus all the way from Maryland to Missouri. People would stare at me, then turn away as soon as I made eye contact. I kept my hat pulled down over the left side of my face. My hair had grown back in some but was bare in places. My eyelid hung down over my eye and was almost all the way closed.

I arrived in Springdale in the afternoon. It was cold and windy as I took a cab over and checked into the VA hospital. I still needed some skin grafts, and some nerve damage that needed to be repaired.

Vick and Sis came to see me as soon as I got settled. Sis was badly shaken when she saw me. She hugged me and couldn't quit crying. I told them not to tell Mom I was back. They told me she was sick, and in a care center, that I should go see her. She had just given up after Dad died. I asked about Mary and they said they didn't know where she was.

I said, "I will find them."

Vick said, "Let it go, Danny. It's over!"

CHAPTER V

"You know, Mr. Watts, that you are the third one of you people from the street, which have been beaten and brought in here this week. The police are waiting to talk with you. I told them it would be morning before you can answer any questions. You are going to have some mighty sore ribs and I think you have a bruised kidney. You got worked over pretty good. We will put a cast on your hand, it is only a hairline break, but I don't want you using it for a few weeks. We will keep you here until tomorrow and then transfer you over to the VA hospital. Your eye that was burned was swollen pretty bad, and I want their specialist to have a look at it. Also, the packing in your nose should remain there until the swelling starts to come out of it. I will send a report over with you, and Danny, find a new part of town to hang out in."

I had a rough night trying to breathe with my plugged nose and my ribs bruised like they were. Even the pain pills didn't help. I lay there trying not to move and thought of all the nights I had spent in a hospital bed. I had survived Nam, and now the damn punks on the street were trying to kill me. The more I thought about it the madder I became. I made up my mind there and then that I wasn't going to take getting pushed around anymore. The bank had taken the farm that I had worked on with my father, and this took his life. My friend had taken my wife and daughter, and now the punks were taking my right to walk the streets.

Morning finally dragged by and the police came to talk to me. They asked about the attack and if I had done anything to provoke it. They wanted to know if I knew any of my attackers or had seen them before.

"I recognized one of the boys as the one I hit with the bottle over on Chestnut, and maybe the one that ran was there also. They seemed to know me, as one of them kept saying, 'This is the one that hit you with the bottle.'"

"We have had a lot of you homeless boys being beaten lately. The word on the street is they call it 'bum bashing.' Someone is going to get seriously hurt or killed if this keeps up, but they all seem to have good alibis. Even their parents lie for them."

I really didn't feel like talking. My nose hurt and I had trouble swallowing. It was hell to get up and use the bathroom. The pain in my ribs cut short every breath I took. Why these young men took a disliking to us I had no idea. I did know that as soon as I got out of there and healed up, someone else was going to hurt a little. I was damn tired of hurting both mentally and physically.

The officer finally left and said he would contact me if he found out any more about my attackers.

That afternoon I was transferred to the VA hospital. The same young doctor that checked me in before was on duty this time. He said that he was getting a lot of experience just patching me up. Of course, I had to explain everything all over again, and he had to push on every spot that was sore. He did take the packing out of my nose, which was a big relief. He said that they would leave it out unless I started bleeding again. They put me in a room with another man whose head was bandaged up and he looked like he had been beaten worse than me. I didn't try and make conversation for a couple of days I was getting to where I could breathe better and my kidneys and ribs didn't hurt as much. They had put a black patch over my eye, and said they wanted to keep the light out of it. Like this was going to hurt me. Hell, I couldn't see out of it, but I went along with them. I was mad at myself for even getting into this scrape. I should have turned around and went the other way instead of crossing the street. I should have never let them get close enough behind me to kick me in the back. It was that kick to the kidneys that took me down. It almost paralyzed me for a while. There must have been a dozen of them, and they were on me too quick for me to run.

There were people that saw this attack on me, and no one offered to help. I don't know who called the police, but they took their own sweet time in getting there. It seemed like they would never stop kicking me. No one seems to care about homeless people. I think they would all like to just shut their eyes and make us go away.

I had been in the room for about five days, before the guy in the other bed said anything.

One morning he raised up and said, "Hi. What in the hell happened?"

"Which time?" I asked.

"The last time I guess."

"I got the hell beaten out of me by a bunch of street punks. How about yourself?"

"It must have been the same bunch that got me. I don't remember much about it, as I was pretty drunk at the time. All I can remember is some people beating me with sticks and kicking me. Telling me I had better get my homeless ass out of town and stay out." "Sounds like the same bunch that got me."

We talked for a while, and I found out he had been in Nam. He had been in several fire fights and had come home unscratched; all except for his mind.

"They call me 'Mad Mike' on the street," he said. "I can get pretty crazy when I am using. I am ok if I am sober, but these doctors would like to lock me up someplace. Sometimes I think some of them are nuttier than I am. I got into the hard drugs in Nam. The damn stuff was everywhere and I figured I could handle it. I was hooked before I knew it and I burned my brain on the damn stuff. They had me in the looney bin after I came back. I finally convinced them I wasn't any danger to anyone."

Mike told me he knew of a couple other people that had been beaten up by these gangs of punks.

"Maybe we should get some of the boys together and set them straight," I said.

"Hell, man, the shape we're in we couldn't whip an old woman in a wheel chair."

"We could change that too, look what we have been through. If we can't kick ass on a bunch of teenage punks, we deserve to get our ass kicked."

"Do you think we could really find enough guys that would fight?" "Let's put the word out and see what we can find out."

Mike and I planned on this all the time we were in there. We would sit and look at a city map figuring out escape routes, and places we could run that the police couldn't drive to. We talked about this every day. I got a map of the city and marked where we both were attacked. They were only two blocks apart. We need to find the other men that were hurt and see where their attacks took place. I got permission to leave the hospital overnight. I stopped by the mission and talked to Bob. He was concerned about the beatings that had happened. I stayed for the service, as I needed to talk to some of the men.

We got a bottle and met in the alley. I discussed what Mike and I had planned. I asked them to put the word out. We would meet on Sunday at the little park on the hospital grounds. That way no one would get suspicious of what we were up to. About thirty people showed up. I explained that all we were going to do was whip some ass and teach these punks a lesson. We had to do it in a military manner, and everyone was to stay sober and clean. No weapons other than clubs and sticks were to be used and no one was to be struck above the waist.

We were each to plan a path of escape and an alternate plan. Also, each had to secure themselves an alibi if possible. This was to take place at the park over by Battlefield. That way we could escape through the pedestrian tunnel that goes under the express way. This park was one of their favorite hangouts. We planned this for the Saturday night before the big cross-town football game, as some of the guys involved were jocks, and liked to brag about men they had beaten.

All day long men drifted into and around the park trying to stay out of sight, and not draw attention to themselves. As darkness fell a couple of the men sat on a bench out by the street and pretended to be drinking. Soon several car loads of punks drove by and threw stuff and cussed them. The trap was set and baited.

Shortly after dark we could hear them coming. The two men got up and walked to the picnic shelter. About a dozen young boys showed up and started threatening them. Before they realized it, about forty of the meanest-looking men I ever saw had them surrounded. They soon realized that they were in deep shit. You could hear a whimper from some of them. One mouth in the crowd tried to sound tough, but a board across the shin bones put him down in the dirt, crying and begging like a baby. Some of the others were pale and pleading their case.

One at a time they were bent over a table, their pants removed, and their bare ass beaten black and blue. By this time they were crying and begging; some were even puking. *Whatever happened to the tough bunch that had beaten me?* Some even wanted their mommy's.

Mad Mike took out his knife and said, "Let's castrate them." This I put a stop to, but he cut off the bottom of one's scrotum, then another, until about half of them were bleeding pretty bad.

"Let's see you wear a jock strap on that next week, pretty boy," he said. "And the next one of us that gets beaten, we will de nut every one of you little bastards."

"Let's split!" I said, and with that we all faded away into the night. Mike and I headed back for the hospital, but not before we stopped for a jug. We had slipped our clothes out in a laundry bag that we had stashed. We changed back into our hospital pj's and robes. We were back into the ward before anyone knew we were gone.

We couldn't wait to see what the local news would say about this or what kind of stories those young punks would tell. Morning came and I wanted to be on the street. Only Mike and I just laid around the hospital recreation room. We watched a ballgame on the tube and caught a little of the local news. There was some mention of some boys being injured in a gang fight, but they didn't give any details.

Monday morning, Sergeant Pool from the city police showed up. He wanted to talk to me. We met in a private room. He said that some of the boys that had beaten me were attacked by a bunch of men on Saturday night, and wanted to know what I knew about it.

I said it couldn't have happened to a nicer bunch, and that I had slept the whole night at the hospital. "Best night's sleep I have had since those little bastards worked me over," I said. If I knew anything I sure wasn't going to tell him.

He really blew up! He got in my face and said, "We would have eventually gotten those guys and you know it. We won't have a bunch of has-been veterans and vigilantes running around town dispelling their own form of justice, and if I can prove any of you were in on it, I will lock your ass up and throw away the key." "Sounds like you have a real problem, Sarge." "This better be the end of it," he said.

"Why tell me? Sounds like you better give that message to those little punks."

"Those little punks, as you refer to them, just happen to be the sons of some of the most prominent families in town, and the chief wants some butts for this."

"Yea! I bet he does. I'll bet he felt the same way when some of us boys got worked over too. Hell, I'll bet he can't sleep at night for worrying about it. Like they say in Nam, Sarge. 'What goes around comes around.' I paid my dues to this country and you can see what I have to show for it. Take a good look," and I pulled my patch off my eye, and asked, "how in the hell would you like to look at this every time you looked in a mirror."

"It's my job to protect every citizen," he said. "I can't pick and choose. The law is the law, and without it we have total anarchy."

"Yea, and without men like me getting our ass shot off for it, where would we be?"

"Look, Mr. Watts, I didn't come here to argue politics with you. Here's my card. If you hear anything, would you call me?" "You bet," I said. He knew damn well I was lying.

After he was gone, I got to thinking of what we had done. We traumatized some of those boys pretty bad. I should have never let Mike cut any of them. I don't know that I could have stopped him, but I sure should have tried harder.

I was discharged from the hospital the following day and was back on the street. I never saw Mad Mike after that. I was dried out pretty good so the craving for a drink was gone. The weather was warming up fast so the need for shelter wasn't as bad as during the cold nights.

I spent the day just lying around the park. Mostly just watching people come and go, especially the kids. This, of course, brought me back to thinking about Mary and my little girl. Why all this had to happen, I could not even begin to figure out. I thought she loved me, like I loved her. Someday I would figure out a way to see my daughter, and to care for her, but now I just have to get my mind and body in order.

One good thing had come from the beating. It had gotten the doctors interested in doing some reconstruction surgery on my face. I have to go back in a couple of weeks and see a specialist.

The afternoon wore on into evening and I thought of going over to the mission. As I walked over to Division Street my thoughts turned to Bob, and how he would receive us after we had the little go-around with the local boys.

The services were just starting, so I walked in and took a seat near the back. It was basically the same message on how faith in God would make everything right. My faith must have been lacking somewhere as things sure as hell weren't right with my life. After the service and the evening meal, Bob sought me out and asked to talk.

We went into his office and he poured us each a hot cup of coffee. He asked how I had been and how I was doing. We talked for several minutes, then the conversation turned to the fight we had with the young boys. Bob didn't think too well of us getting revenge on them.

"Dan," he said, "the people that donate the money to run this place are some of the parents of those boys."

"That might be, but it doesn't give them the right to kick us around. They could have killed or crippled us. Some of us were severely beaten by them."

"I want you to take it easy, and all of you to keep a low profile until this blow's over. Whipping those boys was one thing, but cutting a slit in their scrotum was another matter. Some of the fathers are ready to come looking for you guys with guns."

"Well, I'll bet those little bastards will think twice before jumping one of us again."

"Dan, violence only brings violence. The police would have handled it. I had been talking with them and they had talked to several people that come in here."

I slept at the mission that night, and stayed and helped Bob with breakfast, and the clean up afterwards. It was hot and humid when I left the mission. I walked over toward the park on Battlefield Rd. There is a river that runs south of there. I walked down to the stream and out onto a gravel bar. I sat and threw rocks into the water until I became tired of that. It was a nice warm day and no one was around. I walked down stream on the river for several miles. It started to get dark in the southwest and I knew I was going to get awfully wet. Lightning was flashing all around, and the clap of thunder would make your head hurt.

The rain hit all at once. I was soaked to the skin before I could find shelter. I was afraid to get under the trees due to the lightning, which was striking closer all the time. I saw an old barn across the field so I made a run for it. The barn was old and a lot of the roof had blown off. I found a dry corner where some hay bales were stacked. I was soaked and shaking from the cold. I moved some of the bales to make a wind break, and opening one, I spread the hay out in a loose pile and crawled under as much of it as I could. I lay there and shook uncontrollably. The storm lasted several hours and darkness came so I decided to stay there.

HOMELESS

I was cold and hungry, but it was five miles or more to town and I wasn't about to walk that far in this rain.

Sleep finally came. I was dreaming about Nam, some soldiers were chasing me. I could never get my weapon to fire and I couldn't out run them. Suddenly, I was awakened by a loud explosion of thunder. Fear filled every pore of my body. I lie there shaking and confused as to where I was, then lightning flashed again. I thought I saw someone come into the barn, but I wasn't sure. I lay there scared and cold. Had I seen someone or not?

I held my breath and waited for the next lightning flash. I saw movement and could hear walking. Who or what was in there with me? Did they know I was there? The sound came closer and I felt one of the bales move. I was frozen with feal'. I felt around for a board or stick, anything I could use for a weapon. Just then a loud clap of thunder made me jump half out of my skin. Then a long flash of lightning lit up the whole barn and a cow coughed at the same time. I almost came unglued. Several more cattle came into the barn. I felt a little more secure, as the hay I stacked up kept us separated, and I went back to sleep.

Morning came and with it a beautiful day. The grass sparkled with last night's raindrops. I walked back to the river and it was running high and muddy. I stood and watched a tree float by and several old logs. Then I headed back up stream toward town. By the time I hit Battlefield Road my feet were soaked from the wet grass and my clothes were still damp from the night before. I was broke and hungry. I headed for Commercial Street, and the post office.

The postal box held a note from Vick saying that Mom had passed away, and the funeral was going to be on Friday. He also left me twenty dollars, and my VA check was there. I asked the clerk what day it was and he said Thursday. I cashed my check at one of those gyp joints that charges you ten bucks to cash it. Mom was to be buried at the battlefield cemetery which was close by.

I made my way up town and bought some new clothes and a few toilet articles. Then I went over to the YMCA. I rented a room and took a good, long, hot shower. I trimmed up my beard and with the patch on my eye I didn't look too bad. I didn't look too good either. I was pale and had lost weight. I dressed and went out to a restaurant and ordered a steak dinner with all the trimmings.

The meal was good, but by then I needed a drink. I knew better than to start drinking again, but I bought a bottle anyway. I lay there in my room and thought about Mom and all the hardship she had gone through. The whisky warmed me and soon I was asleep.

Morning came early and I lay there listening to the movement of people about the building. I got up and took another hot shower, letting the heat from the water relax every muscle. I thought about the funeral and realized I didn't know what time it would be. It didn't matter if I was on time anyway for I wouldn't stand with the rest. I now had an extra set of clothes and nothing to carry them in. I took a pillowcase from the room across the hall. The door was left open and no one was around. I also took a towel and wash cloth. I put my clothes and toilet articles in it. I also took both extra rolls of toilet paper from my room and the other one; also the two little bars of soap and a shower cap. I figured I paid for it so why not use it.

I left out the back way and walked over to the cemetery. They were only set up for one grave so I supposed that would be Mom's. I stashed the pillow case in some bushes and walked over to where a large monument was and sat down. Then fear gripped me! What if Mary showed up? She always thought a lot of my mother. If I saw her I would just stay out of sight. Besides, I didn't want people to see me. They always ask such stupid embarrassing questions. Maybe some of them didn't know about my injury, but still they could show some respect.

I had been there a couple of hours when I saw the hearse, and a long line of cars turning into the cemetery. I wanted to leave. I didn't want to be part of this, but out of respect for my mother I stayed. My brother Vick and his wife, and Sis and her family, all got out of the first car. I guessed the three young girls and old couple as Vick's daughters and his wife's folks. I recognized some of the others, as friends of my mom and dad. A couple of the families were neighbors from when we had the farm. The rest I had no idea who they were.

The service was short and the people had started to leave when Vick saw me. I tried to get out of sight. He walked over to where I was and we talked. He said they hadn't lowered the coffin yet, if I wanted to see Mom, it wasn't too late.

"No! That's ok. I went over and saw her at the rest home several weeks ago. I want to remember her as she was then."

Vicks wife came over and then the three girls. I was attracting a crowd! That I didn't want. The girls kept looking at my face and it really made me nervous. Vick introduced me to his family, and the little girl gave me a hug and said, "I always wanted to meet my Uncle Dan." This filled me with emotions that I didn't know I had. They wanted me to go with them but I declined, saying I wanted a few minutes alone with Mom.

After everyone was gone, I walked to the grave and stood looking at all the flowers. I read some of the cards and remembered some of the people. I could still remember how tight Mom used to hug me when I was waiting to go into the Army. I guess I should have visited her more often. All this was gone now. My feelings overwhelmed me, and the tears began to fall. As I stood there shaking with grief, I heard a car door slam. I turned and there was Maty, Artie and a beautiful little girl. I wanted to run, but I just stood there looking at the little girl, who was staring at the man with the patch on his eye, not knowing I was her father.

CHAPTER VI

Vick had said it was over. Would it ever be over for me? Could I ever forget or forgive. Didn't I have a right both moral and legal to see my daughter? To get to know her, to hold her and to be a father to her. I know that my looks would scare the child. But must I always see her from a distance? Hell, I hadn't even done that.

I had returned from Viet Nam with a broken body and a broken spirit. Did my heart have to remain broken also?

They had held a ceremony at the VA hospital and pinned six medals on me, then read a script about my heroic deeds. There was no one from my family or any of my hometown friends there to hear a word of it. I left the hospital with several skin grafts pending. I wanted to see my daughter and for her to have the medals I had received. I walked the streets and slept in the alleyways and old buildings. I hunted the phone books in every small town looking for Artie Johnson's name. He and Mary and my daughter seemed to have left the area.

I was standing in front of the mission when I saw Artie drive by one day, so I knew he was still around. I finally got a city directory and there he was. His name and address. They lived on the outskirts of town, but he was listed and his place of employment.

My search was over. But now what did I do? I hired a cab one day to drive me by the place they lived, just hoping Mary and my daughter would be out where I could see them. I couldn't bear to face her. I don't believe I could take the rejection that I knew would come with it. I stayed in that part of town and slept in every open building I could find. I walked past the house a dozen different times and never saw anyone. I carried the box with my medals and some photographs of me in it. All I wanted was to give them to Mary and ask her to give them to my daughter.

Finally one morning I saw her and the little girl go into the house just as I turned the corner about a block away. I went to the house and knocked on the door. She opened the door then slammed it in my face. I pleaded, "For God's sake, Mary, just talk to me a minute. All I want to do is see my little girl. I don't even know her name."

"Just leave, Dan, your face is so hideous that you would scare her. Now leave or I will call the police."

"I am not leaving until I see her."

I sat down on the porch and didn't move. It wasn't long until a county sheriff named Hill showed up. He told me to stand up and put my hands behind my back.

"Why?" I asked. "You don't even know why I'm here and you are not cuffing me until we talk."

He grabbed me and pushed me toward the porch rail. I turned and struck him hard in the face. His knees buckled and he went backwards a few steps. He pulled a nightstick from his belt and jabbed at me with it. I could see fear in his eyes and a trickle of blood ran down the corner of his mouth. I knew I was going to jail anyway so I thought I would make a show of it. I swung a left hand wide and he used the stick to block it. I stepped in and hit him with a straight right hand and down he went. I was standing over him when the other cars pulled up. Mary must have called for more help.

I walked toward the first officer that got out of his car. He was ordering me to get on the ground.

"I said shoot me, you yellow bastard. I am as good as dead anyway."

Something hit me on my blind side and the whole world exploded in my ear. I did manage to land one more punch on one of them. Then the mace hit me. I was blinded and couldn't breathe and wanted to puke. My eyes were on fire, especially the blind one. It wouldn't make many tears so it wouldn't flush itself. They put the cuffs on me so tight that I thought they would cut off my hands. I was dragged to a car and thrown into the back seat. My face was on fire. I asked for some water to wash my injured eye with. I was told: "You asked for it so enjoy it."

"At least loosen the damn cuffs."

"Just suffer a little, tough boy."

I could see my box of medals and pictures lying scattered on the lawn. Is this what I fought for? I asked myself. Is this the way America repays its soldiers? I just hoped that Mary would pick the stuff up and save it for my daughter.

I was taken to the county jail where I was finger printed and read my rights.

"Screw my rights!" I said. "I got the shit shot out of me fighting for those damn rights and what has it got me? All I wanted to do was see my daughter. She is over three years old and I don't even know her name. Tell me more about my rights."

"They don't give you the right to beat a police officer," he said. "He didn't have any business pushing me around and threatening me without just cause. He didn't even ask why I was there. I am sorry I hit him. I have always tried to respect and obey the law, but he asked for it!"

I was thrown in a cell with three other men. They wanted to talk! I didn't. I crawled into a bunk and went to sleep after soaking my eye in gallons of water. The next morning my bad eye was swollen, and the place on the side of my face that had been burned was one ugly blister. They loaded me in a patrol car and took me to the hospital in cuffs and a belly chain. Like I was some hardened criminal.

The emergency room doctor asked me what happened, and I told him the whole damn dime novel. I said they emptied two cans of mace in my face because I busted one of their smart-ass buddies. He flushed my eye and filled it with some ointment, that made it feel a lot better.

He told the cop, "You should have brought him in last night.

Mace and burnt tissue have an allergic reaction. It states that on the pamphlet that comes with it. You boys are open for a good law suit. I will have to file a report on this, just in case something comes up later on."

The officer asked me why I didn't complain last night.

"I don't usually bathe in mace. All I know is that was the way I was supposed to feel. Don't worry, I'm not going to sue anyone, but I might ask for a little less time."

"That will be up to the judge. You will see him this afternoon."

I went before the judge that afternoon. Some grouchy-looking old fart that looked like he got up on the wrong side of the bed. He told me I was charged with disorderly conduct and striking an officer. How did I wish to plead? I tried to explain, but he just said, "We're not here to hear the case, just to hear a plea."

I had three choices: guilty, not guilty, and no contest. He explained the latter, so that was what I pleaded. First the officer told his story, about how I became violent as soon as he arrived, and that I had struck and kicked him.

Then it was my turn. I tried to explain that I had just gotten out of the VA hospital and went to see my daughter, and my wife wouldn't let me see her.

I was told that there was legal recourse within the law to handle such matters.

"And where do I get the money to hire an attorney?" I asked. I told how the officer immediately told me to stand up and put my hands behind my back, without even asking what I was doing, or why I was there. That he shoved me toward the porch rail, and I felt threatened so I struck back.

I also told about all the mace sprayed on me. And the refusal of the officer to allow me to wash it out of my injured eye. I explained that I didn't have any tear ducts in that eye, and that I had to be taken to the emergency room the next day. I told him how I suffered all night, and several times asked for help, and was told to just wash it with water.

"Your honor, just look at my face, it is still red and swollen. That is from a reaction to mace sprayed on a burn scar that is not fully healed."

I lied a little, but I thought it might help my case if I became more of a victim. I explained how I was wounded in Viet Nam fighting for my country. How my wife deserted me, and the fact that I had not been allowed to see my daughter. That I didn't even know her name.

"Mr. Watts," the judge said. "Your country appreciates the sacrifices that you have made for it. However, we cannot in any way condone the fact that you struck a police officer, while he was in the performance of his duty. Therefore, I sentence you to ninety days in the county jail."

With that done, I was transported to the county jail where I was stripped and searched. Then told me to shower and given a pair of coveralls and a pair of slippers.

I was led through several hallways with bars and gates on them and placed in a cell with no windows. The cell door was shut and I was left alone to ponder my fate. Anyway, I wouldn't have to look for a place to sleep or panhandle a meal for the next ninety days. Hell, these bastards were doing me a service! With that thought in mind, I crawled up on the top bunk and went to sleep.

The meals weren't much but were filling, and although I hate to admit it, they were a lot more than I had been used too. Most of the prisoners in my ward were drunk drivers and college kids that had been arrested for protesting the war. One of them made the mistake of calling me a baby killer. I grabbed him by the throat and pulled him up close to my face, and told him to, "Take a good look, you long-haired maggot, no baby done this to me." I grabbed a handful of hair and slammed his face into the wall. Someone hollered for a guard and said they had a man down. When the guard arrived, he asked what happened, and everyone said he tripped and fell, that ended anyone messing with me.

I had been in there a couple of weeks when I was told I had a visitor. Who would be visiting me? No one knew I was there except maybe Mary! I was escorted to the visiting room, and there stood Artie. There was a screen between us, and he still looked like he had seen a ghost.

"I had to come, Dan," he said. "I couldn't live with myself any longer. I am truly sorry, man. I don't know how all this happened."

"Well, if you don't, and I don't. Who in the hell does?" I said. "I used to think you were the greatest guy in the world. Man, I loved you like a brother. I would have laid down my life for you, and all you can say is that you're sorry? You're sorry, all right, you are about the sorriest bastard I ever knew. I bet your family is sure proud of you. What other great things have you done? Stand on the corner and hold a peace sign?" I asked.

"Look, Dan, I deserve every bit of this. I came here because I felt someone owes you an explanation. You know I always wanted Mary." "Well, you got her," I said. "Can't you handle it?"

"Please just let me talk, Dan. Mary was heartbroken when you left. She was so sick while carrying Danielle."

I sat there with tears streaming down my face. I said, "Finally, after five years, I've found out what my daughter's name is."

"God, Danny! I had no idea that you didn't know. This is very difficult for me."

"Yea it's just peaches and cream for me too."

"Dan, just let me talk. Please!"

I sat there in total silence, not hearing half of what he was saying. I have never in my life felt so much hate for anyone as I did at that moment. He tried to explain how all he was trying to do was help Mary. That somehow things got all mixed up and the next thing he knew they were living together.

"I am so sorry, Danny. I didn't mean for this to happen."

"Are you finished?"

"No," he said, "there is one more thing. I want to adopt Danielle. "Get the hell out of here," I said, "If I could get through this damn screen, I would rip your ugly face off. You will never adopt my daughter. What do you think she is, an animal that is for trade and barter? She is my flesh and blood. She may not know that I am her father but someday she will."

"Danny, she thinks I am her father!"

The shock of those words hit me like a hammer. I had never thought they wouldn't tell her who her father was. I sat there in silence, too stunned to even think. I was glad that there was a screen in front of us. I promised God I would never kill another person, and I do believe at that time, if I could have reached him, I would have tried.

I finally regained control of my emotions, and I said, "Artie, you and Mary have a problem. I will come for my daughter someday and I will come with a truckload of lawyers. I may have to wait until she is old enough to understand, but it will happen. I was in Nam when you took advantage of the situation. I had to hear things from my brother. It felt like someone had torn my guts out. Here I was thousands of miles away and my wife leaves me. There wasn't a thing I could do but hurt. Artie, I left a box of medals on your lawn. When you get home look through them and you will find a Silver Star that I was awarded for bravery. Take it and pin it on your shirt. For you to come here, you have more balls than a stud bull. Wear it proudly. Now get the hell out of here and don't ever come back! And tell my daughter that her daddy is coming for her."

I was physically drained when I returned to my cell; my nerves were gone. I shook all over. I would have given anything for a drink. I lay on my cot for hours just thinking. I had to get out of there and find some way to make enough money to get a lawyer. I made plans to get back to the hospital and get all of the reconstructive surgery on my face that I could. I now had a reason to live and her name was Danielle.

I would go back to school. I had the GI bill and some money for college that I could get through the veterans' administration. Tomorrow I would call the public defender's office and ask for help in getting an early release. I would call the VA hospital and ask to be readmitted. I lay there and couldn't sleep. For the first time in years I had the desire to live. Morning finally came, and I was determined to start my life over. I would get to be with my daughter or die in the process.

I hurried through breakfast such as it was, and waited for my turn on the phone. I called the public defender's office and told them my tales of woe. They said they would send someone out to talk to me within the next few days. In the meantime, I called the VA hospital and talked to the doctor's nurse. They had me scheduled for constructive surgery on my ear. I explained that I was in jail, for a minor offense, and asked if they could help get me out. I had already been there thirty-nine days.

On Thursday I was told I had a visitor. It was a young girl from the defender's office. She had read my case report. She asked me about it. I told her the whole sad story. About my arrest, the mace and the trip to the hospital the next day. Also about the pending surgery I had at the VA hospital. She said she thought they could get me released.

Monday morning I was taken to the jail office, given back my clothes and belongings, and released into the custody of the public defender's office. The girl from the defender's office took me to lunch where we met another attorney, by the name of Sloan, from 'Sloan and associates.' He asked me if I wanted to pursue the mace incident and being denied medical treatment.

I was told if I would it would save someone else from suffering the same treatment. I really didn't want any part of it but told him to see what he could do. I went with him to his office and signed a couple of papers and left. It was getting late in the evening and I didn't have any place to sleep so I walked over to the mission. There was scarcely anyone there. Bob was glad to see me. I told him about finding out my daughter's name, and the way it all came about. I also told him I was going to go back to school and try to get to visit her. I stayed the night and helped Bob serve breakfast again the next morning.

After breakfast I cleaned up the kitchen while Bob did some mentoring with a couple of men. I took a cab over to the VA hospital and made an appointment to see my doctor. Only thing was it would be two weeks before I could see him. Leaving the hospital, I walked along Battlefield Road to the cemetery and stopped at Mom 's grave. All the flowers had been removed, and now it was just a mound of dirt. I stood there a long time just looking at the grave. Finally, I said, "I am sorry, Mom, I know I made some bad decisions that cost all of us dearly. But I promise you that from now on I will try and make things as right as I can." I left and walked down to the river. I slept there on the grassy bank that night.

Come morning I still had a few dollars. So I walked to a little café over on the south side and had breakfast. I sat there in the booth for well over an hour just trying to get my mind straight. This was the longest I had been sober in years. I didn't know what to do with myself. I bought a paper and walked over to Grant Park, sat on a bench in the warm sun and read it. I even went through the help wanted ads. I thought there might be a night watchman job or something. I could do that, I wouldn't have to meet a lot of people.

I stayed there in the park most of the day. Usually I would be drunk by now or at least have a good buzz on. Then fear gripped me, could Artie some way without my permission adopt my daughter? What if they moved to another state, could I find them?

I needed to talk to an attorney, but I didn't have any money. I thought about Sloan and decided to go to his office. It was a long walk over there and I knew it would be too late today to make it. I needed a place to sleep, and I thought about the old guy at the boiler room from the city hospital. It was only about a mile or so from the park so I walked over there. It had been a couple years since I had been there. Would he remember me?

The old blue Ford was still parked by the smoke stack, so I figured he was still there. I walked over and the door was open so I stepped inside. It was hot as could be in there. Albert was bent over pulling clinkers out of the furnace. The back of his shirt was wet with sweat. I watched him work, finally he turned and saw me.

"Have a seat," he shouted, above the roar of the furnace. "I will be up in a minute."

I moved a chair over by the big open door to where it was cooler. Soon he came up the steps from the furnace, beads of perspiration were running down his face. He stuck his hand out, and as we shook hands, he said, "Where have you been?"

We sat and talked for a while. I told him about all I had been through. He got out his thermos and poured us some coffee.

"Want a sandwich?" he asked, then laughed and said, "I got bologna and cheese this time. You don't have to eat eggs tonight."

I was hungry, but I declined. I still had a few dollars so I would eat later.

While we were sitting there talking, three young men walked by dressed in white. "Got a bunch of new doctors," he said. "They come here and serve their internship, then move on to a bigger hospital someplace else."

Something about the movement of one of them caught my eye as they walked into the building. I thought, Could that be Carson? Had he survived?

CHAPTER VII

I sat and talked with the old man in the furnace room for a while longer. I couldn't get the movement of the young doctor out of my mind. Could that have been Carson? He had been shot all to hell the last I had seen of him. I can't believe he could live through that.

Albert got up to stoke the furnace and I just drifted out the door without saying goodbye. I walked the streets for a long time, not knowing where I was going or even really giving a damn. It staffed to rain a cold, miserable downpour that looked like it would last all night. I was too far across town to go to the mission, so I started looking for a place to sleep.

There was a big house close to the street and I noticed that there was an open crawl space underneath. It was a high foundation and you could almost stoop enough to get under it. I decided I would slip under the house until it quit raining. It was dusty and dirty, but at least it was dry and warm. There was a roll of old carpet shoved into a corner and I unrolled part of it and made a good bed. I could hear the people moving around in the house above me. There were children laughing and playing games. It made me want for a family of my own. I got to thinking of Mary and my daughter again.

Would I ever get to be with her? I finally drifted off to sleep. I had some weird dreams. I hoped I didn't wake the people up that lived there.

I awoke early when I heard someone stirring around in the house.

It was dark and still raining when I slipped out and started down the street; to where, I didn't have any idea. I found a little restaurant that was open over on National Street, went in and ordered breakfast. No one paid much attention to me. I was just another bum off the street who might have enough money for a meal. I stayed in the restaurant for a couple hours hoping the rain would quit.

After I left the restaurant, I walked up toward the square in the middle of the old town. It was the holiday season and everyone was putting up Christmas decorations. I thought how good it would be to be in a home with a family and a tree and all the wrapped gifts. Like it used to be when I was a kid.

People hurried without noticing me. I was just a homeless soul with a patch over my eye. I walked the streets just looking at the decorations and the window displays. How I yearned for a family, just someone to love, to hug, and hold. I needed a woman. How long had it been since I had felt the softness of a woman? I ached for the company of the opposite sex, for sex itself. It had been so long that the daily urges were almost gone. Just the basic survival needs were all that seemed to matter now, and at times I didn't really care. I had lain sick for days in cold, wet places not knowing if I would live or die. Not really caring, I had given up on life itself. The wine helped ease the pain of the loneliness, but the effect of it was really taking a toll. My teeth were starting to go bad and my stomach was starting to protrude due to the lack of proper nourishment. Even my mind was being affected; I would walk and talk to myself, not making sense. I was angry with everyone and everything. Loneliness will do that to you. You feel that you are lost in a sea of people. Most will not even make eye contact with you. They will shy away like you are some vermin-infested creature.

Sundays are the worst of all. I would walk by a church and stop and listen to the singing and the sermons. If I tried to go in, the very people who were there to do the Lord's work would lead me outside. They would take a stray dog in and feed it but not a homeless person. If each church in town just took in one homeless soul there wouldn't be enough of us to go around.

Many people I have met on the street are a danger to themselves. Some are beyond help with extreme mental problems. Others are there because they just need a helping hand, or someone to care for them and to believe in them. I wanted the same thing, as most people, and I believed I could have it, but first I had to gain my own self-respect and the respect of others.

I walked on over to the park and watched some young boys with kites. I hadn't flown a kite since before high school. It looked like fun. I stayed there until almost dark, and then started walking toward the Frisco Yard, figuring I would spend the night in the jungle there. I had just come across the tracks when a police car pulled up and told me to get in.

"Why?" I asked.

They told me I was trespassing on railroad property.

"If I am, everyone else around here is too." I got in the car and they took me to the station and put me in the tank with a hundred other drunks and derelicts. I protested bitterly but to no avail. Anyway, I had a warm, smelly place to spend the night.

Morning came and they fed us some cold oatmeal and made us take a shower. Then they set us free. A waste of the taxpayers' money, but I guess they didn't waste that much. I don't believe they ever got around to checking to see who I was. The police do this once in awhile just to see who is out there, and to make us stay away from places we shouldn't be at. On extremely cold nights, this saves some people from freezing and suffering from frostbite.

I walked over to the mission and helped Bob with the noon meal. I stayed the day there and helped clean up the place and spent the night. I sure didn't want to spend another night in the tank. I left after the morning services were over, walked over to the post office and checked the mailbox I shared with my brother. I had a note from Vick and he left me twenty dollars. I also had a check from the VA so I was in the greens for a few days.

There was a place over on Boonville Street that cashed checks for you, for a ten percent fee. I cashed the check and bought some clean clothes and a package of underwear. I rented a room at the YMCA for the night. Took a shower and slept between clean sheets for a change. I stayed in the room until check-out time, then sat in the lobby and read a magazine until after dark. I didn't want to spend the money for another night at the Y, so I drifted over to the hospital and sat in a waiting room that was vacant. I later lay on a couch and slept the night.

I went down to the cafeteria and had breakfast. No one paid any attention to me. It was snowing hard outside so I just moved up to another waiting room and got comfortable. I spent the whole day there, drinking coffee that was furnished and reading until my eye hurt. That evening I walked out back and talked with Albert for several hours. He let me sack out, back of the furnace again. When his relief came, he introduced me to him and he let me spend the rest of the night there.

Morning came and I moved out after thanking the man. The snow was about five inches deep and frozen stiff. I knew the mission would be full, so I walked over to the bus depot, and went into the café there and had breakfast. I stayed there for a couple hours then moved out into the lobby and pretended to read and sleep. I had to leave in the afternoon and just walked around for a time. The new clothes I had bought were heavy and warm. I had wool socks and heavy boots, so my feet stayed warm and dry.

I drifted over to the park and was going to sleep under the skating ring again. I hadn't been there for a long time and after dark I walked around to the back of the building. Someone had boarded up the crawl space so I couldn't get in. I was in trouble. The mission was full and it was going to get below zero tonight. I bought a bottle of cheap whisky. I didn't really want a drink, but I figured it might help get me through the night.

There was an old cave over the hill by the lower end of the park. I walked back down to it and forced my way through the screen that was closing it off. I felt my way back into the cave and it got warmer as I went farther back into it. I had no light and I couldn't tell what was in the cave. It was wet in there but it was a lot warmer than outside, so I spent a dark miserable night. Even the whisky didn't make the rock floor any softer. It seemed like morning would never come. I could hear the squeaking of rats, and felt things run across my body.

I left there early in the morning and went over to the little café on Division Street. The skinny waitress was still there. Like myself she hadn't gotten any better looking, and her disposition hadn't changed any either. I had a breakfast of hotcakes and eggs, washed down by the worst coffee I ever tried to swallow. I sat there in the booth for several hours sipping that awful coffee and watching people go by.

The people on the street had started referring to me as 'Patch Eye Dan' or just 'Patch.' I didn't really care. The only time I associated with most of them was either at the mission or in the jungle around a fire. Sometimes I got so lonely that I would seek out some place where other men hang out just to hear a human voice and to talk a little to someone.

There were a few homeless women on the street. Most of them were so strung out on drugs that their minds were gone. Most everyone stayed shy of them. They would try and prostitute themselves when they needed money. Most were so old and dirty that no one would touch them. It is hard to believe, but most homeless people have a few morals.

I worked my way back over to the mission. There were a bunch of young people in front talking to everyone that would listen to them. They asked me if I had a few minutes to talk.

"Hell," I said, "I got forever, if I live that long."

The girls were sort of cute but dressed in the hippy fashions. They asked if I would take part in their war protest over at the college.

I said, "I did my war protesting in Vietnam. That's how I lost the eye."

We talked some more, and they wanted to know about me being wounded, and how long I had been in Nam and about my stay in the military hospital.

They invited me to go with them over to the college coffee shop. I went along, for lack of anything else to do. We went to the college cafeteria and ate our fill. The food was free. All you had to do was get a tray and take what you wanted. I liked this already. We walked up to a large dormitory building. The lobby was full of people with signs. They were protesting L.B.J., the war, and America in general.

I asked some of them what they really knew about the war in Vietnam. All I got was some dumb looks then someone said, "Man, we know it is wrong and they are killing babies."

I said, "It's wrong alright, but the Viet Kong are the baby killers, not the Americans." For a moment I thought I was going to get an old fashion butt whipping. These punks didn't want to know the truth; they were just fired up to raise hell. I was asked to give a speech on the terrible things that our soldiers did over there. I wasn't about to put down our troops, but I played along just to see what would happen next.

Someone lit up a joint and passed it around. I took a hit and passed it on. I was hoping to spend the night with one of the young hippie chicks that seemed to be everywhere. I spent the night with about twenty young girls and boys with sleeping bags there in the lobby of the dorm. Every girl I put the move on just pushed me away. Hell, it was warm and I had slept in worse places so I finally quit trying and went to sleep.

Come morning we went to the cafeteria and ate all the free breakfast we wanted. Then everyone went over to the front of the college and started parading around hollering and raising hell. I was offered five hundred dollars to make a speech against the war. I asked who was paying for it. And some dude said, "Who cares, all the money for this comes from some foreign government. We get paid to go from college to college and set up these demonstrations. Hell, if we get thrown in jail, we have a get-out-of-jail-free card. All we have to do is call this number." He gave me a card with a name and phone number on it. It was some guy in New York who had a foreign name I couldn't pronounce.

I spent the day there just watching the show. We had another free lunch at the cafeteria and I decided I would spend more time at college. I was beginning to like the college life if this was what it was all about. I wandered all around the place and no one even took a second look at me. All the college cops were sitting in vehicles watching the kids do their thing.

I detested the speeches about the war and decided I better get out of here before I said or did the wrong thing. At least I knew where I could get a good meal anytime, I wanted it. The 'good old college crowd, 'dumb as owl crap, but well educated. I moved on over toward the mission. I came past the cemetery where we had buried Mom. And I started thinking of my meeting with Mary. It was all like a bad dream.

CHAPTER VIII

We all stood there like we were frozen in time. I turned to walk away and Mary said, "Wait! Please wait! We need to talk."

As I turned around, Artie took the little girl by the hand and walked back toward the car. Mary came up to me and placed her hand on my arm. I stood there shaking with emotion. As I looked into those beautiful blue eyes, some of the hate in me melted away.

I wanted to grab her, and hold her, and never let go. At the same time, the years of hurt were flooding my mind; the thoughts of her being with another man; the letter I received from my brother while I was in Nam, the God-awful, sickening hurt. The total feeling of helplessness and being told by Vick while I was lying wounded in a hospital that she was living with Artie. Not even being told anything about my daughter. Here in front of me holding onto my arm was the one person I loved and hated the most! All wrapped up in a beautiful package.

I wanted to scream. I wanted to cry. Finally, I just said, "Why, Mary? Why? What did I do to deserve all of this?"

She stood there crying, holding onto my arm. I wanted to be cruel, I wanted to hurt her to cause her some of the pain I had been through in the past five years. She still wore the same perfume, her odor made me yearn with desire. I wanted to take her from this place, away from here, and everyone. Just to be alone with her, to love her, to hold her, and smell her hair and body.

"Danny, I am so sorry. I never meant for any of this to happen. You were gone for so long. I lay and cried for you every night. My days were filled with worry about you and wanting you near me. I needed someone and Artie was always there. He would make me laugh. He took away the tears. I named our daughter after you, so that you would always be remembered, and in my mind. Every time I call her name, I think of you. Oh, Danny, I have caused you so much hurt. Is there any chance of you forgiving me?"

I sure wasn't ready for this. All I had ever thought of was revenge. Tears were running down her face. Her mouth was trembling. God, how I wanted to kiss those lips, and to wipe away those tears. I reached out and pulled her close to me. I pressed my face to her head and smelled the aroma of her hair. She shook uncontrollably.

"I love you, Mary. I always have, and I always will. Some way this will all work out. Take care of our little girl and tell her who her real daddy is."

With this said, I turned and walked toward the back of the cemetery. I retrieved the pillowcase with my spare clothes in it and walked away. I never looked back. My mind and emotions were a total wreck. I bought a bottle of wine and headed for the jungle.

There were several men sitting around a smoking fire.

"May I join you?" I asked. I opened the bottle and took a long drink, then passed it to one of them. I sat there for hours just listening to them talk. My mind kept returning to the cemetery and Mary. Had I done the right thing? Had the things I'd said and done had any impact on her?

She had never said how she felt about me, just that she was sorry for the hurt and pain she had caused me.

Artie at least had the smarts to stay away from me. Could I ever forgive and forget? Only time would tell. I passed the bottle on when it came back around. My days of lying around drunk were behind me. Some way I was going to get myself back. I owed it to my daughter and I owed it to myself. I spent the night there in the hobo jungle behind the old Frisco railroad yards. I told myself if I ever came here again, it would be to help someone else get out of there.

With the morning came a new feeling, and a new challenge for life. I still had seven days until I went back to the hospital. I just decided to let God and life lead the way. I walked back to the river and decided to walk down stream for a mile or two. I eventually came past the old barn that I had spent the stormy night in. I had to laugh to myself when I thought of how bad that old cow had scared me.

The field was being plowed, and I noticed someone working on a tractor by the edge of the field. I walked over and asked if I could help. A woman that was dressed in men's clothes jumped when I spoke. She was almost in tears.

"It just quit," she said.

"Let me have a look at it. I used to know a little about machinery." The gas filter was plugged and the sediment bowl was full of dirt. I cleaned it and just took the gas filter out of the line, pushed a screwdriver through it and put it back on. I crawled up on the tractor and with a couple cranks of the starter it was running good.

"Thank you ever so much," she said.

I introduced myself and explained to her that I was waiting to get into the Veterans Hospital. I was getting some reconstructive surgery done on my face. I told her I would finish plowing the field for her, in exchange for a home cooked meal. She pondered on that for a moment. Then said, "You got a deal."

I put the tractor in gear and started the rounds on the field. I watched her walk across the field toward the house. She was a woman about thirty-five. She looked to be put together pretty good, but with those men's clothes on it was hard to tell.

God, it felt good to be back on a tractor, with the smell of the freshly turned earth and the smell of the gas exhaust. My mind took a complete rest, as I made round after round of the field, the pull of the engine as the three blades of the plow sliced through the ground. I became aware of the insects and wildlife that the tractor scared up. At last I was back doing what I felt cut out to do. I don't know how long I had been making rounds on the field. I looked up and the lady was standing at the fence waving at me. I shut the tractor down and jumped off and walked over to her.

"I can tell you have done a bit of farming before. You plow a good field. Supper is almost ready. You can wash up just inside the porch. There is a bathroom there."

The house was a standard ranch style, with a large kitchen and open dining area. It was neat and well furnished. I hadn't been in a home like this in a long time. I went into the bathroom and one look in the mirror brought me back to reality. The only white place on my face was under my patch. I washed up as best I could and borrowed a comb that was laying there. My hair was dirty and hard to comb. I did the best I could with what I had and let it go at that. The aroma of food coming from the kitchen made my mouth water.

I said, "I guess I should introduce myself. I am Danny Watts. I was raised over at Arco, Missouri."

"My name is Gloria, come on in and seat yourself." The meal was roast beef and all the trimmings.

"I cooked it in a Crockpot all day, I hope it is eatable."

"It has been a long time since I sat at a real table, everything looks delicious."

She said grace, and we talked all through the meal. I told her all about Viet Nam and getting wounded, and all the time I spent in the hospital, and the surgery I had pending.

I didn't mention anything about Mary or my daughter. I told her I wanted to go back to school, if I could ever get a face that people could stand to look at.

She took a long look at me and said, "Don't be too hard on yourself. You look like a man that has been around is all." Then she laughed. It was a pretty laugh, one that made me feel good inside and set me at ease. After dinner, I offered to help with the dishes. She asked if I would take a look at her lawn mower instead.

I can't get it started. I guess I am just not mechanically inclined." The rubber gas line on the mower was broken and leaking gas. I was able to cut it off and still use it so I got the mower running and mowed part of the lawn, until I ran out of gas. She came out and I asked if she had more gas, and explained what I did to the mower. She walked over and sat at a table that was there in the lawn.

"You have done enough for today come and sit awhile. Where are you living?"

I was embarrassed but didn't want to lie to her, so I said, "Most anyplace I can find. To tell you the truth I have been living on the streets for the past five years." She acted nervous after I said that. "1 need a job and a place to stay."

"I can't afford to hire anyone," she said. "It has really been hard since my husband was killed. He had enough insurance to pay off the farm, but I had to borrow operation money. I wanted to put that forty acres you are plowing into alfalfa, but the bank said I had to put in a cash crop. So corn it is. I know I should sell this place but it belonged to my folks, we bought it from them, and I would like it to stay in the family."

"Would you let me stay a week, and work for my room and board?" "I really don't know anything about you," she said, "but you seem to be good with the machinery."

I told her about being raised on a farm and farming with my father. I said, "Anytime you want me to go, I will be gone in a heartbeat. I am tired of living on the street. I want to do something with my life. I realize I have been living in self-pity for too long and blaming it on everyone else."

She said, "I will try you for a week."

I could have hugged her and would have liked to!

"There are living quarters in pan of the garage. It is just a bed and bath. You can put your things in there. I will get you some towels and stuff." All I had was the clothes and toilet articles I had bought. They were stashed in the pillowcase. She showed me the room. It was a lot more than I had had for the past five years.

"There are still a couple hours of daylight left, I think I will circle that field some more before dark."

It felt good to sit in a tractor seat again. I plowed until it got dark. I loved the evenings in the country. There was an abundance of wildlife everywhere. Two deer ran across the field, and there seemed to be rabbits everywhere. I could hear bob white quail calling. Everything seemed to be so alive. I had been dead to life for so long, it was a real awakening. Every one of my senses seemed to come alive at once. I wanted to live, to grow and to enjoy life to its fullest. I pulled the tractor into the yard and filled it with fuel. I wanted to get an early start come morning.

Gloria came out and had a tray with cookies and iced tea. "I thought you might use a snack before turning in," she said. "You are going to spoil me if you keep this up."

"I am not used to eating on a regular basis," I said.

We sat and talked for a while.

"I think I will take a shower and turn in," I said.

"There are some of my husband's old clothes in the dresser. If you want, you may help yourself too them."

The shower felt good and I stood there and soaked up the heat for a long time. I shaved, brushed my teeth, and changed into some clean underwear that I had. It felt good to be stretched out on the bed. I pulled up the blanket and the next thing I knew it was morning.

I had no idea what time it was and there wasn't any sound coming from the house. So I walked out, fired up the tractor, and resumed plowing. I had the field almost done when I saw Gloria standing at the fence, waving to me. I shut the tractor down and walked over.

"Want some breakfast?" she asked.

After breakfast, I finished plowing the field, then hooked onto a disc plow and spent the morning working the field down so we could plant.

Gloria went to town for seed corn, and I finished up the field. By the time she returned I had the planter hooked up and ready to go. She had stopped and gotten Chinese food, so we had dinner outside on the picnic table. It was getting late in the day so I spent some time fixing a post in the yard fence and repairing a barn door. We sat and talked for a while. She told me about her husband being killed in an auto accident on the interstate.

"He has been gone for two years now," she said. "I still wake up at night reaching for him. He was a kind and gentle man. We never had any children. The Lord just never seemed to bless us that way." I thought of telling her about Danielle, then changed my mind.

All this could wait until I knew her better. I excused myself and headed for the shower. I was tired but sleep wouldn't come. I lay there thinking of Mary and the day at the cemetery. How good she smelled and the softness of her hair! God, I loved her so much, but in turn I hated her for what she had done to me! And Artie! Did he really think I would let him adopt my daughter? Would she ever learn who her father was? Would I ever get to hold her and talk with her and be a father to her?

Working on the fam again had put life back into me. I started making plans and dreams. Some way I would get back what was mine. I had to get my face fixed and get an education so I could earn some money. I figured it would take five or six years, but I wasn't going to wait that long to talk to my daughter. She was going to know I was her father and that I loved her.

Sleep finally came and the morning was there too quickly. After a quick breakfast, I filled up the grain drill and started drilling corn. There was a small pond in the adjacent field. I stopped and took a quick dip in it too cool off. I worked the rest of the day with my shirt off. I should have known better. It took most of the day to complete the drilling.

Afterwards, I serviced the tractor and checked out several other pieces of machinery that she was going to need. I realized that I had a severe sunburn, so I asked Gloria if she had some lotion, I could put on it. She came out of the house and, said, "Take off your shirt" I sat down on a bench and removed my shirt. The lotion felt good on my back and the touch of a woman's hands really sent shivers through my mind and body. I reached up and grasped her hands and pulled her close to me. She stood there for a moment, and then pulled away. "No, Danny! Not yet!"

"I am sorry!" I said. "I understand."

"Don't take this wrong, Dan, your looks have nothing to do with it. You may look a little rough on the outside, but on the inside, you are the most beautiful person I know. I have watched you move and work, the time you take to watch a wild animal and to pick and smell a flower. The way you handle machinery. You have a way with animals, they respond to you. In the week you have been here I have never heard you swear or raise your voice. A woman notices these things about a man. It is just too soon!"

"It's ok. I have waited for the right woman for over five years now, a few more weeks or months won't hurt."

"Thank you, Danny Watts. You are a good man."

The week went by too fast and on Sunday I asked Gloria to drive me to the VA hospital. I asked if I could leave my clothes there, in hopes that I could come back after surgery. I liked this lady and wanted to spend more time with her.

I checked into the VA hospital and met with a Dr. Stephen. He checked out my eye and ear and told me what they planned on doing. He explained how they would take some gristle from the side of my hand and graft it onto the top of my ear. He assured me that it would look somewhat natural, that he could take some skin from my hip and graft it onto the scar on the side of my face and take hair plugs from back on my neck and fix me a hairline.

He said, "You will look good enough that the ladies will be chasing you again."

"All I want, doc, is to look good enough that I don't scare my little girl."

They took me into surgery the next morning, and by evening I was back in a recovery room. My face was bandaged up so that I couldn't see. I realized that someone was holding onto my hand. I squeezed their hand and asked who it was.

"I couldn't stay away, Dan. You deserve to have someone here with you." It was Gloria! I tried to talk but was so sedated that I kept drifting off to sleep. When I awoke the room was quiet, and it seemed dark, but I couldn't tell as both eyes were covered with bandages.

The side of my face stung like it had been scrapped. Then I became aware of the burning on my ear. The burning turned to a hurt. I lay there wondering what this would all turn out to look like. Out of the last five years I had spent nearly two of them in some hospital, and I still had all of the surgery to be done on my eye. The doctors had assured me that that would go fast and heal quickly. I didn't see Dr. Stephen for a couple of days.

He came in and they changed my bandage. I got a look at myself. I have to admit it didn't look like much. The side of my face was real pink. Almost like raw flesh and there was a big purple knot on top of my ear.

"After the graft takes and the swelling goes down, we will shape the ear to match your other one. Then we will transplant the hair plugs. After that, Danny, the eye surgeons get their crack at you.

Within six months it will be hard to tell that you were ever wounded. "Yea right," I said.

"We took pictures of before, and we will take more when we are done. Then we will see what you think."

That night I lay there and thought of all those lonely miserable nights on the street. Days had gone by that I couldn't remember anything for the cheap wine I had drank. I realized that I was blaming the world for my problems instead of facing up to them. I had begged for money from strangers and slept under people's houses without them knowing I was there. I had taken bottles away from crippled-up old men. It was my own fault that I wasted those days. I could have had all this over with if it hadn't been for self-pity.

I awoke early and my ear hurt so much I could hardly take the pain. I rang a nurse and she said the doctor would be by soon.

"It's now, that I am concerned with," I said. She gave me a pain pill. It must have been a good one as it was two in the afternoon before I awoke! Doctor Stephen came in and asked if I had a good nap. He removed the bandage on my ear and looked at it.

"The pain is coming from the nerves in the lower ear, the graft is growing on to them. It will hurt for a few days. If it gets unbearable, just call the nurse. I don't want you on too much pain medication. As I can see from your records, you have had a problem with it."

"That's all behind me, doc. As soon as I get out of here, I am going back to college. I have a little girl out there that doesn't know I exist. That's all going to change!"

Gloria somehow found time to come visit me each day. I got to where I eagerly awaited her visits. The thoughts of Mary were not as painful or frequent now. I really liked this woman and wanted to be with her. I had been in the hospital now for three weeks and Gloria showed up one Sunday morning and asked if I would like to go for a ride. I was still in my hospital pajamas and robe when she picked me up in front of the hospital. We drove around town, then out to the farm.

"I want to show you something," she said. We drove over to the field I had planted earlier and the new corn was just starting to show. "Just look how neat and straight those rows are!" she said. "I could never have gotten them that straight."

"It takes lots of practice," I said.

The drive back to the hospital was quiet. I could tell she was thinking hard about something. She drove me to the side entrance and parked the car. I started to get out and she said, "Wait!" She reached over and pulled me to her and gave me the most electrifying kiss I ever had. Before I could react, she said, "Now get out of here, Danny Boy, and get well quick. I'll see you tomorrow."

CHAPTER IX

I walked back towards my room in deep thought. I was completely unaware of my surroundings. "Good evening, Mr. Watts," a nurse said. It startled me!

"Sorry," I said, "I was thinking about something."

"Yes! I'll bet you were, I was outside when the lady dropped you off. I can see why you would be." She laughed and walked on.

I made my way back to my room, took a shower and sacked out. Morning came a damp, dreary day. I tried to watch the tube, but nothing caught my interest. My face and ear were starting to itch, and I kept rubbing the bandages until my ear hurt again. The doctor wouldn't be back to see me until tomorrow. I finally got up and walked down to the cafeteria and got a cup of coffee and a Danish. I walked over and sat at a table by the window. I was sitting there thinking about Gloria and the kiss she gave me. I really wondered where all this was going to lead me. That day I walked out of the hobo jungle over by the Frisco yards, I had asked God to lead me to a better life. The path I had chosen was leading me to an early grave. I had cursed God and my country. I laid blame on everything and everyone around me. The day I struck the deputy, it wasn't him I was hitting; it was the whole mixed-up mess. I was trying to fight life itself. I was growing insane on the street with no one to talk with. Humans need other humans. We need someone to touch, and talk to, someone to depend on us, and to be able to depend on them. All of this I cried out for, I sought out companionship, but when I got close to someone, I rejected them. I used my ugliness that was on the outside to become ugly on the inside.

That night the boys attacked me I wanted to kill. I wanted to kill Artie. I lay in a drunken stupor many nights and plotted ways to kill him, just to get Mary back. I sat there letting this run through my mind. Could I ever get it straight? Could they really give me back some sort of looks? Would I ever be myself again? I hadn't laughed for so long I had forgotten how.

Gloria had really stirred my hormones into motion with that kiss. I wanted a woman more as each day went by. I even thought of checking out and seeing if I could find a cab driver that knew a prostitute; only I didn't want it that way, I wanted someone that wanted me. It had to be someone I could give pleasure too as well as enjoy it myself. My time would come!

The cafeteria was getting crowded, and I heard a familiar voice. I sat there trying to recognize the voice. I turned to see who it was and there were three young doctors sitting across the room from me. I sat and looked at them. One in particular! I was filled with every emotion a person can experience. There in front of me sat Doc Carson.

I was spell bound. Tears filled my eyes (the one that wasn't bandaged anyway). The last time I saw him, he was covered with blood and lying lifeless on a stretcher in Nam. I slowly got to my feet and walked over to him.

"Is it you, Doc?" I asked. He came up out of the chair like a rocket. You could hear him yell clear across the whole the cafeteria. He grabbed me and picked me up. Tears were streaming down his face. He was hugging me so tight I couldn't breathe.

"Where in the hell did you come from? They told me you were killed that day in Nam."

"Not quite! They tried to blow my head off, while I was dragging your butt to the chopper. They are still trying to put me back together. So you finally made it through medical school, did you?"

"Not yet, I am serving my internship here at the city hospital."

The other two doctors excused themselves, and we sat and talked half the afternoon.

I told him about Mary and my little girl, and how I had been living on the street all these years.

"You will never live there again," he said "Not as long as I live. If you hadn't carried me that day, I would still be lying out there in the elephant grass in Nam. I owe you my life, Dan. We lost a whole damn squad out there. Most of C Company were either killed or wounded. They lost four choppers trying to evacuate those men. Some of them still aren't accounted for. They told me you went out on the other chopper and it didn't come back. I just assumed that you were lost."

"I was!" I said. "Lost to the streets of America. There are hundreds of men out there on the streets that can't go home."

"I better check in," he said, getting up. "What room are you in? I will drop by tomorrow to see you."

HOMELESS

When I got to my room, Gloria was sitting there reading. "Where have you been? I was getting ready to send the orderly out to look for you."

I told her all about Doc Carson and meeting him in the cafeteria. "Small world, isn't it?" she said.

"Not if you are living on the street. It is a big, cruel, lonely world."

"Danny, you have got to put all of that behind you," she said. "It is in your past, learn from it. Don't let it pull you back down."

"I need to talk about it, to tell someone of the horror and suffering that I went through, to get it out in the open. Then maybe I can let it go."

"Anytime you want to talk, Dan, I will be here and I am willing to listen." Then she leaned over and kissed me.

"You do that again and I will have to shut the door!"

She laughed and reached out with her foot and kicked the door closed. She kissed me again, long and hard. My bluff had been called.

I folded my hand.

"Not in here. We can wait," I said. "I don't like interruptions."

She kissed me again. I had forgotten how warm and soft a woman's lips are. It had been a long time since I had touched a woman and smelled the warmness of them. God, I wanted her. When will I get out of here?

Gloria stood up and said she had some chores to do, that she would see me tomorrow. She kissed me goodbye and said for me to behave myself while she was gone. I wondered: did this lady really care for me? Or was she just trying to build my self-esteem? If that was the case she had a good start; I had never felt this good since before I was wounded. I wanted more of life now. I wanted to own things, to get a car, to drive again, and to go see the things I have never seen before. I wanted to go fishing and maybe hunting, although I doubted if I could shoot anything. I wanted a wife and family. I wanted friends, people to party with, and to have back yard barbecues with.

It felt good to want things again. I wanted children. I wanted my daughter! I want to buy her pretty dresses and to play games with her, to show her how to do things. I called my brother Vick. It had been so long since I called him he didn't know my voice. We talked for a long time. I told him about my surgery and about Gloria, and my plans to get off the street.

He said, "I wondered how many years it was going to take for you to find yourself. We are all with you, Danny, if you ever need anything just call! Is it all right for us to come visit you?"

"Yes! Anytime," I said. "I will be here for a few more weeks."

"We will see you Sunday afternoon, then. Before I forget, there is a lady from the public defender's office looking for you; also, call Bob over at the mission. I will bring your mail to you. You have three checks from the VA that you haven't picked up. I will keep the notes that I had left for you."

I went to sleep that night full of dreams and plans. I slept better than I had for years. Can I do all the things I am dreaming of doing? Morning came with a pouring rainstorm. One of those Ozark storms that pours down for hours.

HOMELESS

Gloria called and said she couldn't come in today, Things were getting soaked and she had to get some of the machinery under cover. Dr. Stephen showed up shortly after lunch. They took me into a small treatment room and put me in a chair. He said, "Let's see what things look like today, Mr. Watts."

"Please, call me Danny. That mister bit makes me feel old."

The bandages were removed and I sat there listening to the doctors and nurses discussing how things looked. I asked for a mirror so that I could have a look. I was surprised! Where the brown burnt scar had been, now was clear pink skin, and I even still had some of my own hair growing on it! Hell, I even had an ear! It wasn't the prettiest ear I ever seen, but it was an ear.

"We will let this heal for another week or two. Then I will shape the top of the ear. After that we will do the hair transplant, and then the eye doctors can have you." He smeared some ointment onto it and redid the bandage with a smaller one.

That evening Doc Carson showed up and we went to the cafeteria for supper. He apologized for not being up to see me sooner. He said that he had so many classes and reports to do that it was hard to keep up.

We talked about Nam. He said, "I remember getting hit the first time, and seeing you come over and pick me up. It was all like slow motion. I couldn't feel the pain. I couldn't move, I was totally paralyzed. The first round hit me a glancing blow just above my temple." He brushed back his hair and showed me a white scar about two inches long. He laughed and said, "Bounced right off my hard head. I was hit twice more in the back and shoulder. I lost a lot of blood. I guess they just did get to me in time. I read the report on how you were wounded and, in the chopper, then jumped out and came out for me under heavy fire. That was dumb."

"You would have done the same thing."

"Yea, but that was my job. Danny, I owe you my life! You are the best friend I ever had, over there or anywhere."

"To tell you the truth, Doc, that damn door gunner jumped out and saved both our asses. I got my leg shot out from under me as the chopper was lifting off. The door gunner jumped out, and shoved me back aboard, and then he threw you in. They almost took off without any of us. The incoming fire was murder. That damn chopper was full of holes. All I can remember is the blood, it was all over you and me running out the door. We were all shot to hell. I don't know how many wounded were left lying there on the ground. I do know that we left a lot of good men lying out there."

"That damn war should have never happened. Why we got involved in it I will never know, and don't want to know. It was a hell of a place to grow up, but you grew up fast or you didn't grow up at all."

"My mind was so messed up after I got back, I tried to run from life, but my ugly face wouldn't let me. Everywhere I went it was there, reminding me. I bet the wineries had to put on a double shift after I hit the street."

We sat and talked until late into the night. When I finally turned in, I was asleep in seconds.

Morning came and it was still raining. I waited for Gloria to show up or call. I had lunch in the cafeteria. After lunch, I sat and watched it rain for a couple hours. I never heard from her all day. I thought she had probably changed her mind about me. I really liked that woman. She was eight years older than me, but that didn't matter. I still wanted her.

I went back to my room and tried to sleep. Why hadn't Gloria called? Had she been injured or had a change of heart? My phone rang and I almost jumped out of bed. It was Gloria. She was in tears and could hardly talk.

"The river is up over part of the corn and is still rising. I have to have that cash crop this year or default on my note at the bank."

I tried to comfort her. I said, "We will manage somehow." How did I get to be part of this? I wondered. Six weeks ago I was a bum looking for a place to sleep. Now I was worrying how to help save a lady's crop. I told her that it will stop raining pretty soon and the river would recede. "The corn will be ok! It can take a little flooding, as long as it doesn't wash too much silt up over the crown. Go to bed and get some sleep and come see me tomorrow. My brother and family will be here for lunch."

Sunday was a beautiful Ozark day; the rain had quit sometime in the night. I wondered how bad the corn got flooded. It would make it hard on her, but farming is a risky business. It is hard on everyone.

I walked down and had coffee and toast for breakfast. There were only a few people in the cafeteria. Sunday mornings are usually pretty quiet, people either get up and go to the chapel for Sunday worship, or sleep in a little later. I picked up a Sunday paper and took it back to my room. It bothered me to read with only one eye. I probably should get glasses to help it.

The front page showed a picture of the floodwater over one of the bridges. I wondered if Gloria could even get to town! My brother and his family showed up shortly after lunch. We all walked out to the little park in back of the hospital. Vick had three girls. I had only remembered two. His youngest would be about Danielle's age. She was a real character, even wanted to wear my eye patch, which nearly put Vick in shock. I gave it to her to wear; the two older girls looked at me awhile, then lost interest. I explained to them how I got injured, but they really didn't seem interested.

Vick's wife, Sally, was a real pleasant woman. She liked to talk and kept asking why I had never came to visit them. I tried to explain how I couldn't accept my injury and felt uneasy around other people. "How did you cure that?" she asked.

About that time Gloria came walking up. I introduced her to everyone, and said, "This is the person that cured me. Or at least got me on to the road to recovery."

As it turned out Sally and Gloria knew each other; they had attended elementary school together, and occasionally bumped into each other. We sat and talked all afternoon, while watching the children play and explore the hospital grounds.

Everyone wanted to go eat some place. I said I could go as long as they would let me in wearing pajamas and a robe.

Sally said, "There is a little restaurant just down the street. Lots of patients go there and eat when they get tired of hospital food."

We walked down. It was a nice little place and the food was good. We sat and talked after the meal. The walk back to the hospital was enjoyable. We decided to walk around a different way, as I really needed the exercise. Gloria and Sally seemed to enjoy each other's company as they caught up on old times.

Vick waited until all the women went to the ladies' room then said, "Mary called me the other day. She wants you to call her."

I thought about this for a while. Vick gave me the phone numbers to call.

The ladies came back from the rest room and little Audrey gave me back my eye patch. Mom must have said something to her. She gave me a kiss on the cheek and said, "I am sorry, Uncle Danny." I assured her it was all right. She was such a cute kid. I wondered what Danielle looked like now. It had been over a year since I saw her at the cemetery.

It was such an enjoyable day. I even found myself laughing, something I thought I had forgotten how to do.

Vick and his family soon left, assuring me that they would be back next Sunday. If I left the hospital, I was to call them. Gloria and I sat and talked awhile. I wanted to get back out to the farm; only, I was scheduled for more surgery on my ear the next day. It would only be minor, and I might be able to get outpatient status for a couple of days.

Gloria walked me up to my room and stayed a while longer. She gave me a big hug and a kiss, and said, "Hang in there, tough guy, I'll see you tomorrow."

I lay there wondering what Mary wanted, and the attorney, Sloan, what did he want? Could it be that they were trying to adopt Danielle? I also needed to call Bob over at the mission. This coming in off the street was a bigger job than I thought! Hell, I need a secretary. I finally drifted off to sleep. Morning came and I wasn't allowed breakfast due to the pending surgery. Funny how I could go days without eating while I was on the street. Now I couldn't miss one meal without getting hungry.

The nurse came in and prepped me for surgery. They took me in about ten and I was only in there a little over an hour. When I came around, my ear hurt like it was on fire. The doctor said it was because of the awakening of the nerves and the cutting he did to the new tissue. They offered me a pain pill but I refused, and said, "1 can live with it."

Gloria showed up that evening and said that we lost maybe five acres of the corn. But she thought that the rest would make it, if the weeds didn't take it first. I asked the doctor about getting outpatient status for a few days.

He said, "Let's wait a day or two and see how things look by then. You sure don't want to get infection in that new surgery. It could undo all we have accomplished."

That evening I called Bob at the mission. He said that several people had been looking for me. "A lawyer named Sloan, and a girl from the public defender's office. And I think it was your ex-wife that called. I am not sure about that though. Also, Sergeant Pool from the city police was asking about you. What have you been up to? You are getting to be one popular dude."

I explained about the surgery I was having and told him I would be by to see him soon.

They took the bandages off after a couple of days, and the top of my ear really looked like an ear, even though it was red and swollen. It still had several stitches in it. Doc said they would remove the stitches in a few days, and then things would look a lot better.

Doc Carson stopped by and said he had stood in and watched my surgery, and I was lucky to have such a skilled surgeon as Doctor Stephen. I asked him about my eye.

He said, "I am not supposed to be doing this." He shined a light into my eye and pressed on the eyelid, and asked if that had any feeling it.

I pulled back, and said, "Hell yes, so don't go pulling it off!"

He told me that unofficially he thought with a cornea transplant I could see out of that eye again. Reconstructing the eyelid would really take some doing, but he knew people that could do it. And one of them just happened to work for the VA hospital in St. Louis. We would have to wait and see what Doctor Stephen had to say about that.

"You might ask him if he knows an eye specialist by the name of Peil that works for the VA hospital. Don't mention that I said anything though. I wouldn't want any of the doctors thinking an intern was doing something he shouldn't be."

We talked some more, and I told him about the fact that Mary was trying to contact me.

He said, "I would walk a wide circle around that one if I were you, Danny. I have got a meeting to go to, Dan. By the way, when they construct your new eyelid, they use a piece of your foreskin. Works great! But it makes you a little cock eyed." He laughed and went out the door. I thought, some people never change.

When Gloria showed up, I told her about the conversation with Carson. Especially the part about rebuilding my eyelid. She laughed and said, "Don't let them cut too much off. You might just have other needs for it someday."

We walked down to the cafeteria, and Gloria had supper with me. Afterwards we sat and talked and then went for a walk. We walked around the little park behind the hospital and down to a small pond that was there. We stood there for a long time holding onto each other. She smelled of a fragrance that was new to me. It stirred the wanting deep inside me. It felt good to just hold someone. It made me want my life back that much more. God, I had wasted so much of it. I hoped that in some way I would be a better person for all I had been through.

Gloria said that she had gotten the cultivator on the tractor and had gotten part of the corn cultivated. I really didn't want to talk about corn right then. But maybe it was a good idea. I pulled her to me and kissed her long and hard; we just stood there and held each other tight for a long time. She finally said, "We better get back inside, wouldn't want you to catch cold in that ear, now would we. "Wasn't my ear I was thinking about!" I said.

She laughed, that soft gentle laugh of hers. It made me want her more. I think I am falling in love with this lady, I thought. I will have to think more about this.

We walked back up to my room. She stayed and talked a little while longer, then kissed me goodbye and left.

HOMELESS

I lay there thinking until I dozed off. When morning came, I still hadn't solved anything in my mind. I still had people to call. But didn't know why. It was just that I was told they were looking for me. I called Sheri, the girl from the public defender's office. She asked me about the night I was attacked by the gang of boys over on Chesnut Street. She wanted to know about the police dog being turned loose on me.

They had a complaint from a night watchman that saw the officer turn a dog loose on someone after they were lying still. She wanted to know if that was me. I told her it was. She asked if I had done anything to provoke it. I told her I just did what he said. I asked him why, and he said that the dog needed fed or something like that. I told her I wasn't hurt and didn't want to cause any trouble.

"We have had some complaints about a couple of our officers, and we need to correct their behavior, or move them to a new job. ,,She also told me that I needed to contact Sergeant Pool from the city PD I really wasn't interested but wrote down his number anyway. Hell, that damn dog didn't hurt me any. Maybe I gave hill rabies or something! I couldn't be that damn lucky. She also told me that it was very important for me to call Mr. Sloan.

The doctor showed up just before lunch, and they took me into a room and removed the bandage on my face and took the stitches out. Except for being a little pink and swelling some, I looked halfway normal. It looked like the only hair they would have to transplant would be around my ear and on my temple. He replaced the bandage with a smaller one, and said he wanted to see me in three days, that I could go home if I would keep out of the sun, and to keep that bandage clean and dry.

The thought of going home seemed strange to me. I really didn't have a home, but I knew a lady that did. So I called and she wasn't home. I went back to my room, cleaned up the best I could, and put on what clothes I had. I went down to the cafeteria and had a sandwich and a glass of milk.

I went back up to the nurses' station and had her page Doc Carson. He called in and I told him I would be gone until Monday, that I would contact him then. I tried to call Gloria again, but still no answer. I sat in my room until four o'clock and she showed up.

"Ready to go?" she asked.

"How did you know?" She just laughed.

We drove up through town. I wanted to stop for a burger, but Gloria said no, that she had stuff already fixed at home. As we drove into the farmyard, cars came from everywhere honking and people yelling. Scared the hell out of me! I didn't know what was going on. It was a welcome home party for me! There were my sister Viola, brother Vick, Doc Carson and a couple of the nurses that helped me at the hospital; some old neighbors, and a couple of old school buddies I hadn't seen since graduation. Even Bob and a couple guys from the mission were there. I was happy but visibly shaken!

I hadn't been around so many people in a long time. It really made me nervous. I half expected to see Mary and my daughter show up. I guess that would have been a little too much. Sally and Gloria had dreamed this up after the meeting at the hospital. I was a little jumpy but managed to enjoy visiting with everyone. I finally realized these were all people I could have turned to for help. I had turned my back on them, not the other way around. I came out of that damn war totally messed up.

I was worn out by the time everyone left. Gloria told me to go into the bedroom and lie down, that she would clean things up a little. I wanted to help, I even asked her to let it go till morning, but you know women!

I awoke to the sound of thunder and lightning was flashing. I lay there listening to the storm. Gloria came in and asked if I was awake. "I hate storms," she said. "They scare me, and that is when I hate being alone the most."

I said, "I always liked storms if I had a dry place to get out of the rain." I told her about the night I spent in her barn and how the cow scared me. We both laughed, I lay their holding her close to me listening to her breathe. Smelling the cleanliness of her body. I gently stroked her hair. We lay like that all night, both of us sleeping soundly.

When morning arrived, she got up and looking at me said, "Danny Watts, you are truly a gentleman."

CHAPTER X

After breakfast, I walked out to look at the cornfield and the surrounding farm. The corn looked good except for the acreage down by where the river backed up on it. Most of it was about a foot high. I yearned to get on a cultivator and work the ground. I needed to be out in the fresh air, but I couldn't stay out long, as the sun was pretty hot. I headed back to the house and Gloria.

When I got back to the house Gloria was sitting at the picnic table in the yard. She had fixed me a glass of iced tea. We sat and talked for a long time. I watched her as she got up and moved about the lawn pulling weeds and picking flowers. I thanked God for my simple act of kindness that brought me here.

If I hadn't stopped to help her with the tractor that day, there is no telling where I would be. I was just wandering like so many homeless people do, with no place in mind to go, just looking for a place to sleep or eat. She was a beautiful woman in the prime of her life. What attraction she had for me I don't really understand. I only knew I would be as good to her as I possibly could be. I wanted to hold her and to make love to her, but it would be on her terms, I wouldn't push it. I had waited this long, I could wait longer.

The party she had for me had helped me a lot. I am learning to accept myself for who and what I am. I could meet people for the first time in years without trying to hide. I should call Mary and see what she wants, but I was afraid to. Some of the hurt she caused me had gone, but I failed to see how any good could come out of me calling her.

I got up and walked over to where Gloria was pulling grass out of her flowers. She stood up and turned to me smiling. I pulled her close and hugged her to me and thanked her for taking me in. We stood there holding each other. Finally, she spoke.

"You are a good man, Danny Watts. The world has asked a lot of you in the few young years you have been here. The day you fixed the tractor, I was scared of you. I wanted for you to leave, but something pulled me toward you. I had been praying for God to send me someone to help me with the farm, only I was expecting a knight in shining armor. Not a homeless man in rags, with a patch over his eye." She laughed. "You are that knight, Danny, it's just a fact that your armor is dented a little. I plan to hammer out those dents and make it as good as new." With that she gave me a long hard kiss and a hug. "I need to go see the banker today. Do you want to ride along?"

"Yes. I have three checks I need to cash, and I should have a couple more at the post office if you will stop by there."

We drove into Springdale and stopped at a drive-in for lunch. I had forgotten what fast food tasted like. It was the first milkshake I had had since high school. Life was starting to really be good to me and I loved it. I also loved this lady that had helped me so much. I wanted to tell her this, but I was afraid it would scare her away, or ruin the relationship we had. I had nothing to offer her but my scarred up mind and body. I knew that I could still do a day's work and I would work myself to death for her.

We drove over to the post office. I had two more checks there from the VA, also a note from Bob. He wanted to see me. We went to the bank and when I tried to cash the checks the girl asked if I had an account there. I said no, and she talked me into opening one. When she asked for my address, I gave her the post office box number. Gloria overheard me and told me to use her address. This really humbled me. I had to find out how she really felt about me and what plans she had for us. I was getting in too deep. I didn't want to get hurt that way again.

I had given a lot to this world and country that I live in, and had asked for very little in return. All I wanted out of life was to be able to work and have a wife and family, and to be as close to normal as I could be.

The teller at the bank brought me back to reality when she said, "Sign here." I kept a couple hundred dollars in cash and put the rest in a checking account. I had them put Gloria's name on the account so she could draw out of it also. We went to a couple clothing stores and I bought some underclothing and a shirt and a couple pail' of jeans. I had been wearing some of Gloria's husband's old clothes. They fit all right, but I needed stuff of my own. We drove over to the mission, and I introduced Gloria to Bob.

"Now I see why you haven't been around, Dan," he said. "You need to get in touch with lawyer Sloan. He calls here every day asking for you. Also, your ex-wife keeps calling here looking for you."

Gloria turned and stared at me with a look that needed lots of answers.

"We have got to have a long talk," I said.

"Yes, and the sooner the better."

"Let's go to a diner someplace where it is quiet so we can and eat and talk."

She said, "I am not so sure I can eat right now."

So we drove over to the cemetery where Mom was buried. We got out of the car and walked around. I took her by the hand and told her about my getting married right out of high school, and of going to Viet Nam, getting wounded, and of my little girl being born while I was in the hospital. Also, of never being able to see her except for a glimpse of her at the cemetery when Mom died. About my best friend, Artie, moving in with Mary while I was wounded, and lying in a hospital in Maryland. She was pretty upset.

"Just when were you going to tell me all this? On our wedding - night!" Those words really hit home!

"I was afraid to tell you, afraid that you would tell me to leave. Gloria, I have nothing to offer you. I am just a scarred-up homeless person that helped a lady fix a tractor, and I love that lady so much I couldn't bear to lose her."

She threw both arms around my neck so quick that we almost fell over backwards.

"Oh, Danny! I have been praying that you would say that. I fell in love with you the first day you were here. I have been so afraid that you would just up and leave. I want to be with you forever. I want for us to meet your daughter together, and for her to live with us, or at least spend some time with us."

I kissed her long and hard while standing there by my mother's grave. I said, "Mom, I want you to meet the woman that I am asking to marry me."

Gloria just stood there with tears in her eyes and said, "Well!"

"Well, what," I said

"Well, ask me."

I took her hand and knelt down beside my mother's grave and looked up at the loveliest person I'd ever known and said, "Gloria, will you please marry me?"

She stood there trembling and said, "Danny Watts, I would be honored to marry you."

I was shaking. I was scared. I was happy. I was completely messed up, so I just stood there and held her.

Finally she said, "We have to go tell someone."

We drove around until we found Vick and Sally's house and drove in unannounced. We were both beaming with joy. When we told them, Vick said, "This calls for a drink."

I said, "Make me a soda. I don't use the hard stuff anymore." So we toasted with a glass of cola. "We haven't set a date yet, so we will let you know."

I drove home. It had been the first time I had driven a car in over six years. I didn't have a license, but it didn't matter. I was happy. As we turned onto the farm road, Gloria said, "Dan, I have something I want to tell you."

Now what? I thought.

"Dan, I already knew about your daughter and Mary. Sally told me that day at the hospital. She didn't exactly tell me. She let it slip when she asked if you ever got to see your daughter. I wasn't supposed to tell, but I can't go through life keeping anything from you."

"Same here," I said, "but do you mean to tell me that you let me sweat and squirm all that time over something you already knew. "Got you to propose, didn't it?"

"I would have gotten around to telling you!" I said. "And I would have gotten around to proposing. I think. It may have taken me a year or two, but I would have found the nerve." I reached over and kissed her and said, "But thanks for the help anyway. You know, Gloria, I have to go back to the hospital in the morning. "Yes! I know," she said, "but we still have tonight"

"Speaking of tonight, we still haven't eaten and I am starting to get used to doing that."

I turned the car around and drove over to a restaurant on hwy. 44. We sat and ate and enjoyed a good meal and a good conversation, only I can't remember a word of it. I just kept looking at her and thanking God for my good fortune. The ride home was quiet. Gloria sat close to me and seemed to be in deep thought.

I asked, "Are you getting cold feet?"

"No, I was just wondering if I was too old to have children," she said, and squeezed my leg.

Now I started to get nervous. I tried to joke about it. "Just how many do you plan on?" I asked.

"Oh eight or ten."

"Sounds good to me," and we both laughed.

We got home and did what chores needed doing. I went out to my room and took a shower, being very careful not to get my bandage wet. I changed into a pair of her husband's pajamas. Then I thought, this isn't going to work. She is not going to come to bed with me and me wearing her husband's pajamas. Then another thought came to me. She may not come to bed with me at all! God, I was as nervous as a cat at a dog show. I hadn't been with a woman since Mary, nearly eight years ago. Could I still perform? I just lay back on the bed and decided whatever happens happen!

Soon the door opened, and Gloria came in wearing a robe, her hair still wet from the shower. She sat down on the edge of the bed, and said, "Nice pajamas!"

I thought, oh damn, how could I be so stupid. I told her I was going to take them off. She said, "It's ok. I have seen them before. They look good on you."

I reached out and pulled her to me. She smelled of perfume and she smelled like a woman. I kissed her for a long time. I kissed her hair and along her neck. I was aroused beyond my own expectations. God, I wanted her! Yet something in my mind said this wasn't right. This wasn't the proper time. I continued to rub her body, her skin was so smooth and warm, and she trembled with my every touch. We kissed and caressed one another for a long time. She pressed her body to me.

I asked, "Are you sure?"

She just lay there for a long time, breathing hard, and not saying a word. Finally, she kissed me and said, "Danny, I love you. I know how much a man needs a woman, and I need you too, but I feel cheap this way."

"Gloria, I haven't had anyone since my wife eight years ago. I can wait a few weeks longer." I lay there caressing her body until she was asleep.

I felt proud and like a damn fool at the same time. What had I passed up? What did she think of me? Morning came and I awoke to a completely naked lady lying next to me. I lay their admiring her body, every curve and form of it. I either had to take her or a cold shower, and like a damn fool I chose the shower.

She awoke while I was in the shower. I stepped out completely naked. She just sat there on the bed looking at me. I didn't know what to say, so I just said, "See what you missed."

She laughed and said that it looked different last night. She stood up and hugged me and things started all over again.

She said, "I am sorry, Danny! You can do whatever you want."

I picked her up and put her back on the bed and got over her. I looked her in the eye and said, "Do you always look this good every morning?"

She hugged me tight and said, "Get off me, I have to go fix breakfast. "

She left me there in a daze. Talk about mixed emotions, I had them. This was worse than being shot at. When I get to the hospital my damn blood pressure will be over the boiling point. I thought about choking my chicken but had lost the urge. I got dressed and went into the house. Gloria still just had the robe on, so I walked over behind her, reached around through the robe and squeezed her breast, and tortured myself some more.

"Danny, if you don't stop, I won't be able too."

So like a damn fool I walked over and sat down, and asked, "What's for breakfast?"

As she served my breakfast she leaned over and I could see both breasts, with nipples as hard as I was.

I said, "Go put on some clothes before we do something we shouldn't."

She kissed me and said, "You're a good man, Danny Watts."

CHAPTER XI

We finished breakfast and made things ready to take me back to the hospital. I wanted to get all this surgery over with and get on with living. I had so much going for me now that I didn't want to lose the momentum. The drive to the hospital was an enjoyable trip. We discussed a lot of things, from the corn needing cultivating, to the things that occurred between us the night before. We both thought we did the right thing. I still felt like a damn fool but knew I had done what was right.

I checked in at the hospital and had to put on one of those damn gowns, as I had to go in for an examination. They were scheduled to do some hair plug transplant transfers, which didn't take a whole lot of doing. I met with Dr. Stephen and asked him about Dr. Peil the ophthalmologist. "Where did you hear about him?" he asked.

"From a friend of mine."

"I was going to recommend him to you," he said. "Let me make some phone calls and I will get back to you. It will mean going to St Louis for the surgery and the follow ups."

"That's ok! I just want to get it over with."

"It will take a few days to get things set up," he said.

I asked if I could go home after the hair transplant took place. He didn't see that it would be any problem as long as I wore a hat with a brim on it to keep the sun off and kept the bandages clean and dry. "You will have to come back every three days until the procedure is finished," he said. "It will take about three or four different transplant operations to do it, and by then I should have things set up for your eye surgery."

Gloria stayed at the hospital and waited for me. The hair plug procedure hurt like hell but didn't take long. They only did about twenty plugs. Each one contained about a quarter inch circle of hair. They put a loose bandage on it and let me go.

We drove over to a drive-in and had lunch, then headed for the farm. I remembered that we were supposed to call Mr. Sloan the attorney, so we drove by his office instead. He was in, and after a short wait, we were escorted into his office by his secretary. He stood up shook my hand and said please be seated.

"Mr. Watts, I have been trying to reach you for quite some time. We have filed a suit in your behalf against the county sheriff's office. We are asking for two hundred and eighty thousand dollars for undue pain and suffering and damage to your eye, caused by the careless and negligent use of mace on a burn victim, in the incident that happened to you on June 3 last summer. Also, we are asking for eighty thousand dollars in punitive damages, for lack of immediate medical care after the incident. The county has offered to settle out of court for one hundred and forty thousand dollars, plus they will pay my fees. I strongly urge you to take this settlement. A trial could be long and costly, and we could always lose. Especially if a jury sees you as the aggressor in this incident."

I introduced Gloria to him, as my wife to be, and asked him if we could think this over and discuss it with each other for a day or two. He asked that we discuss it and come back within the hour as this has been pending for quite some time and the county might withdraw their offer.

He said, "Mr. Watts, this is a fair and decent offer. Even though the sheriff's department doesn't admit any guilt, by doing this they do acknowledge that the incident happened."

I looked at Gloria and she smiled at me and said, "It is your decision. That's a lot of money for someone that was broke and homeless a year ago."

"Ok, I'll do it!"

He said, "That's a good decision," and shoved a stack of papers out for me to sign. After I signed all the papers, he picked them up and looked them over and said, "I will call you in a couple weeks. Give my secretary a number where I can reach you." He stood up and shook my hand and said, "If I can ever assist you in any other matters just call me."

"How are you in child custody matters?" I asked

"I don't handle those type of cases, but I will have my secretary give you the number of a friend of mine that specializes in family matters."

"Thank you," I said and walked out to his secretary's desk. I gave her Gloria's number, and she gave me a business card for a 'James A. Black Attorney of Law'

I gave the card to Gloria, and said, "Hang on to this. We may need it sometime."

We drove back to the farm. I found an old hat hanging in the shed and putting it on, I asked Gloria, "Do I look like a farmer now?"

"No!" she said. "More like a pirate."

The cultivator was already attached to the tractor so I drove to the cornfield and started cultivating. It felt good to hear the sound of the tractor and the feel of the cultivator as it plowed alongside the rows of corn. The corn was about sixteen inches high and it looked like a good healthy stand.

I started thinking about Mary, and the times she would ride the tractor with me, and the time Sis almost caught us making love behind the hay bales. Those were good times. All I wanted out of life now was to marry Gloria and get a chance to know my daughter. If I got the money from the settlement, I could at least get the court to rule on my right to see her. I really didn't feel like the county owed me that money, but I guess that is why we have such laws. Most of the police officers were good to homeless people. They kept a lot of guys from freezing to death in the winter by throwing them into the tank. We always seen it as harassment, but in all reality, they were doing us a favor. It dried us out for a couple days and usually got some food in our stomachs. A lot of them even got some medical treatment out of it, if they needed it. They tried to keep us out of certain parts of town, and away from the residential areas. My mind wandered as I plowed; all the way back to when I first drove a tractor for my father. He would stand on the back and give me directions on what to do. Then one day I looked up and he had stepped off and was walking toward the barn. I felt proud and scared at the same time. I remembered how careful I was; I loved operating machinery and didn't want to mess anything up.

It seemed like I had been out there but a short while when I saw Gloria waving for me to come in. I finished up the rows I was working and pulled out at the far end of the field. I noticed a small rabbit run through the corn as I drove to the barn. I thought, little bunny, you better stay in the tall stuff or some hawk will have you for supper. Thinking about supper, I was hungry and hadn't realized it. I was glad Gloria called me in. I parked the tractor and went into the porch and washed up. Supper was only soup and sandwiches but it was delicious, and Gloria had made an apple pie for dessert. The tea was cold and refreshing. After I ate, I took a cold glass of tea and sat out on the picnic table.

The days were getting hot and humid, and the thunderclouds always built up in the evening. It wasn't long until Gloria came out and we sat and watched the storm clouds build. Soon the thunder and lightning was getting close enough that we went inside. It rained for a while but not enough to do much good, just one of those typical Ozark showers that come so frequently during the summer.

Gloria busied herself with work around the kitchen. I got up and walked up behind her and put my arms around her. She turned and kissed me. I stood and held her close to me for a long time. I loved her and wanted her, only we had decided to wait until marriage. We hadn't exactly set a date yet. I had so many things to do. I wanted to wait until I got my eye surgery over with. I would be in St. Louis for a month at least. I finally just kissed her and said,

"There are still a couple hours of daylight left, I am going to work on the corn." I ran the tractor until dark, then brought it in and fueled it, and got everything ready for morning.

I went to the room I was staying in and took a shower and lay down on the bed. I was almost asleep when Gloria came in and snuggled in beside me. I kissed her and said, "Lady, this is where we almost got into trouble last night."

She laughed that beautiful laugh of hers and rubbed my chest and said, "Yea, but it was fun, wasn't it?"

"Was more like pain from my side," I said. "I have been hurting all day."

She said, "I didn't see you trying to get away."

"I was just trying to be polite. You were so turned on that I thought you were going to rape me. "Yea, sure!" she said.

"Someday you are going to have to eat those words, among other things," I said.

We lay there caressing each other until sleep finally came. Sometime during the night she got up and went into the house. I never missed her until I awoke in the morning. I got up and dressed and went into the house. She was up fixing breakfast.

"Lost your nerve again last night, did you?" I said.

"You're the one that went to sleep! I tried to wake you," she laughed.

I walked over and hugged her and said, "I'm awake now!"

"Good, sit down and eat your hotcakes. You got work to do and I wouldn't want you sitting out there on the tractor hurting all day."

HOMELESS

I finished breakfast and got back on the tractor. I felt good. It was great to be alive. This woman really put the life back in me. I had completely forgotten how good it felt to truly love someone. This still all seemed like a dream. Could this really be happening to me? Deep down I had a fear that someday the bubble would break. I tried not to dwell on the negative aspects of life. I had been through enough of that already. So I put my mind at ease and concentrated on the task at hand. When I was finished cultivating, I would hook the disc plows back up, and work up the edge of the cornfield and the lower end that the floodwater got to. We could put in about five acres of milo that still had time to make a crop. I talked to Gloria about this when I came in for lunch.

She said, "I will leave the farming up to you."

I finished the corn shortly after lunch and started to disk the low ground. I worked straight through until dark. I wanted to get all this work done for her before I had to go back to the hospital. I finished the disking and came in after dark. Gloria had supper ready for me so I ate and headed for the shower.

I went straight to bed and would have been asleep in a few moments, only Gloria came in and laid down beside me. I held her close and enjoyed the closeness of her. We talked for a few minutes and I was asleep. She got up and went into the house. I would be glad when we could get married and get over all this foolishness.

Come morning, I called the veterans' administration, and tried to get a new copy of all my papers. I had lost everything while living on the street. All I had was my card from the hospital. I also wrote to the Missouri bureau of public records for a copy of my birth records.

I needed to get two licenses, a driver's license and a marriage license, but first I had to have proof of who I was.

The next morning I had to go back to the hospital. The hair transplants were taking good, so they did about thirty more plugs. Those damn things really hurt. I had a severe headache after they were through. Gloria drove me back to the farm and I laid down and slept until the next morning.

She came in and woke me up and crawled into bed with me. I said, "You could have taken your clothes off first."

She just laughed and said, "It is cold out this morning."

We lay there in each other's arms for a long time. I rolled over and whispered in her ear that a respectable woman would be up and have breakfast ready by now.

She started to get up, but I pulled her back down and kissed her.

Finally she said, "Well, if that is all you have in mind, I have got to get this day started."

I laughed and said, "You don't want to know what I have in mind."

She smiled, "I can guess, and it isn't work."

"Sometimes it can be," I said, "especially if you do it right." I got up and took a quick shower; the side of my head still hurt.

Lawyer Sloan called and said everything was done. I had to sign a couple more papers and the check was mine. It still seemed like I was stealing from someone. The officers that used mace on me were only doing their job and trying to keep me from injuring them. They should have given me something for that bad eye. I shouldn't have been made to lay and suffer all night.

Gloria drove me into town. We stopped at a restaurant and had a late breakfast and an early lunch. We got to the attorney's office about one. I had to sign a bunch of papers that said the sheriff's department was immune to any further action in this matter. Afterwards, Mr. Sloan shook my hand and gave me a check for one hundred and forty thousand dollars. I still felt like I was taking something that wasn't mine.

"Dan, you have suffered for years for this country," Gloria said. "It is time they paid you something for it! You have given everything but your life. Now maybe this will help you get some of it back. Think of your little girl. She deserves something for not having her father all these years." I gave the check to Gloria and asked her to hold onto it for me until I could decide what to do with it.

"I want to set up a college fund for my daughter with part of this journey. When we get home, I am going to call that attorney and set up an appointment. It's time I see my daughter and at least talk to her. My looks don't bother Vick's girls, so they sure as hell shouldn't bother my own."

Gloria said, "Why don't you call Mary and ask to see Danielle? Maybe things have changed. You don't know if they have even told her you are her father."

"She will soon be eight years old. I want to take her something, for her birthday, but I just can't walk into a little girl's life after all these years and expect her not to fear me. I have already waited too long to get acquainted with her."

I found the phone number that Vick had given me. I was shaking while I dialed the number. Artie answered, and my throat was so dry that I could hardly talk.

"This is Danny. May I speak to Mary?"

He didn't say a thing, just hollered for Mary that she was wanted on the phone.

"Hello," she said. "This is Mary."

I stuttered a moment and said, "This is Danny."

She said, "We have been trying to contact you, Danny. We need to talk, face to face, not over the phone. We still want the adoption to go through."

"Not a chance," I said. "Have you ever told her I am her father?" "No, and we're not going to."

"Then we will let the courts handle it," I said and I hung up.

Gloria was sitting there listening, and she got up and hugged me. "Don't give up, Danny, we will get to see her somehow."

CHAPTER XII

I was so depressed, I had to go outside and go for a walk. Gloria got up and came with me. We walked out through the corn and down to the river. We stopped on a gravel bar and I stood and threw rocks into the river. I watched each ripple as it spread out into oblivion. I thought about my life, it seemed like each ripple I made in life just spread out into a bigger wave.

Gloria just remained silent and let me think things through. I looked at her and she seemed more depressed than I was. I couldn't let this happen. I wouldn't let the prettiest and nicest woman I knew get depressed if I could help it. I turned, grabbed her and spun her around, and pretended to throw her into the river.

"It's about time you came out of that gloom," she said.

We walked on over to the back pasture where she had a few head of cattle grazing. The new calves were running around. I thought, how happy all young things seem to be. I had never seen depression in animals, at least not the young. It is only the human race that does this to its young. Why are humans so cruel to their own kind? I thought about the war and all the killing and injuries we inflicted on each other. Surely, God intended for us to be happy and to care for our fellow man. I could not see why Mary never told Danielle that I was her father. If it hadn't been for that day at the cemetery, she wouldn't even know that I existed. How do you tell an eight-year-old that the person she thinks is her father isn't her father? Am I being selfish in wanting to hold my own child? Is it wrong to want her to know that I am her father? I wanted to tell her that I loved her, and wanted to be near her. I wanted to take her places and show her things. Was this asking too much?

I took Gloria by the hand and looked into her eyes, and asked her, "Am I wanting too much? Should I just drop the whole thing?"

"Danny, you are a kind, sweet person. Your daughter deserves to know you, and to know that you are her father. Danny, you didn't cause this problem! Your ex-wife should have told Danielle about you as soon as she was old enough to understand. Now the little girl is going to suffer for someone else's stupidity. There has to be a way to ease you into her life, without causing any trauma to her. We need to go to the state office and talk to someone from the children's agency. Then we can call the attorney if we need to."

I said, "I don't want anything done that will draw that little girl into a courtroom. I won't do that to her." We walked on over toward the pond.

"Want to go for a swim?" I asked.

"You are not supposed to get your bandage wet, remember?"

"That will keep you safer," I said

"We don't have our swim suits."

"We have the ones God gave us."

We stripped off and waded out into the cool, clear water. "You have a beautiful body," I told Gloria as I pulled her to me. We stood neck deep and kissed for a long time.

"You're not too shabby yourself," she said. "Except parts of you seem to shrink in cold water." She laughed at that cute giggle of hers. I forgot all my troubles and just held on to her as long as I could.

"We better get out, before someone see us," she said. "I really don't need a lot of gossip to get started. I can imagine it is bad enough, just having you staying here and working."

"Who would call this working?" I said

She said, "I can change that."

So we got dressed and headed back to the house. I fired up the tractor and drilled the milo, in the five acres around the corn that had gotten flooded out. After I finished that, I hooked up the swather and made several rounds of the alfalfa field. I didn't know how long I would be in the hospital and I wanted to get as much done for Gloria as I could. I checked out the baler and filled it with twine and greased all the fittings. I hated to leave all this work for her, but she had done it before. After supper, I went in and showered and went to bed. Gloria came in and lay there with me until I was asleep. I loved having her close to me and I yearned for the day that we could be man and wife.

Morning came early. I gathered up what toilet articles I would need, and we drove to the hospital and had breakfast at the cafeteria. I was scheduled for the rest of the hair transplants, and then I was to go to St. Louis.

My brother Vick showed up at the hospital about one, so he and Gloria drove me to the VA hospital in St. Louis. I was dreading this and wanting to get it over with also. I checked into the eye clinic at the hospital. Dr. Peil showed up about nine that night and we had a brief consultation about what was to be done to me. After an examination, he decided to fix my eyelid first. I told him about what Doc Carson had said.

He laughed and said, "That is one way to do it. We will strip the scarred tissue from the top of the lid then graft a small piece of skin over it. The thing we have to do is get a piece of skin without any hair follicles in it. Usually the foreskin works the best. We don't have to worry about scar tissue that way."

I said, "Whatever works. Just don't take more than you need."

We both laughed and talked about the eye surgery that was to follow. He said they would peel away the conjunctiva lining with laser surgery. This would remove all the white scar tissue that was covering my burnt cornea. And if there wasn't too much damage to the aqueous humor, they could do a simple cornea transplant. Then I should have vision in that eye again. I would have to wear corrective lens for a year or so, and they would have to be tinted.

The surgery went fine the next day. The eyelid was sewn shut and would have to stay like that for two weeks. I asked if I could go home. Dr. Peil called the hospital in Springdale and made arrangements for me to have the bandages changed there every three days. I called Gloria and told her to meet the bus at five the next day. She was there waiting for me when the bus arrived. We stopped for dinner and went home. I was tired and went to sleep on the couch.

I awoke sometime during the night and couldn't figure out where I was. I got up and started for the room out back where I slept. Gloria called to me and I went in to her bedroom and got in bed with her. She was safe, as things were pretty sore where they took the skin off, but she didn't know that. We lay there and snuggled close to each other and went to sleep. Morning came and neither one of us was in too big of a hurry to get up. I needed to start baling the hay as Gloria had gotten it all swathed. I decided that it needed to dry out more, so I just lay there holding her close to me. I loved the smell of her and the feel of her close to me. The phone rang and jarred us both into reality. It was a friend of Gloria's that worked with troubled children. Gloria had mentioned my problem to her and asked for some advice. She wanted us to have lunch with her that day. I got dressed and ate a piece of toast and headed for the baler.

The wind rows had dried out enough, so I started baling. I baled until about eleven and Gloria came out and got me. I ran in and took a quick shower, and we were in town by twelve. We met her friend Stephanie at the Woodshed Café and talked over lunch. She brought up some interesting points about my rights to see my daughter. I needed to get a copy of her birth certificate and a copy of my divorce decree.

The divorce should have stated what rights I had if any. But first I needed to see if I was listed as the father on the birth records. Mary may have listed Artie as the father if he was with her at the time of birth. If so, they would have to do a blood test to see who the father was.

"Is there any chance that Anie could be the father?" she asked.

This hit me like a sledgehammer! "No! I don't believe that he could be. We were too much in love. Or I was anyway." I could tell Gloria didn't like these questions any better than I did. "Artie was always hanging around. He was my best friend! The thought of him and Mary never entered my mind. He was the best man at my wedding. Maybe he proved it," I said jokingly.

I had to try and relieve the tension that was building up within me. Could Artie have been with Mary? Maybe even before we were married? Was she pregnant with his child when I married her? Hurt was starting to turn to anger, and the two women realized that I was really getting mad. The thought of being played for a sucker was a bit more than I could take. I wanted to know whose child that was and I wanted to know now.

Stephanie said, "Danny, I am sorry I had to bring these things up, but this and a lot more will come up if this goes before a judge."

Gloria was almost in tears. She took my hand and said, "I am sorry, Danny, it seems like the world never stops hurting you."

I needed some air. I asked to be excused and walked out onto the sidewalk. I was almost in tears. I had hated Artie Johnson before, now I bitterly hated him, and Mary, had she really deceived me? I walked for several blocks before I realized I had left them sitting there. I turned and went back to the restaurant. Gloria was sitting there all alone drinking coffee. I had cooled down some, so I walked up and said, "Hi, pretty lady, want to dance."

"Anytime, soldier!" she said.

We left and I drove home. "I've got to get a license one of these days," I said, "or the cops will get me, and with the luck I am having it will be Officer Hill."

Gloria was quiet, finally she said, "That little session really opened up a can of worms. I didn't mean for that to happen, Danny. I just thought Stephanie could help us. She deals in matters like this all the time."

"Maybe it did," I said. "It's better to be ready for something than have it surprise you later on."

It was still early in the day, so I climbed on the tractor and went back to baling hay. My mind wandered as I worked. I tried to remember every time Artie could have been alone with Mary. No! I decided that Danielle was mine; from what I had seen of her she was a Watts. Mary may have gotten to talked into things after I left, but while I was there, I am sure she loved me. I intend to call her and ask for myself. Why would they be trying to adopt Danielle if Artie was listed as the father? There was more to this than was being told. God, would I ever get my life straightened out? That damn war had done a lot more than wreck my body. It had wrecked my marriage and now it was still messing with my mind. I thought about Nam, and all the lonely nights I had to sit out on some listening post. The hot sweaty days and nights patrolling through the rice fields and elephant grass. Every nerve and fiber of your body alert for any movement, your eyes trained on every blade of grass. Just looking for that bent blade of grass that would tell you someone had been there before you. Never touching anything without looking it over twice. Expecting some booby trap to explode in your face at every step. The dead, bloated bodies and the burned-out villages.

Never knowing who the enemy was. Sort of like growing up with a friend like Artie, I thought.

The steady clanking of the baler brought me back to reality. I turned and noticed I had run several bales through the baler without any twine to tie them. I shut the baler down and drove it back to the barn. I got more twine out of the shed and loaded it up. I fueled up the tractor and then went inside.

Gloria was still depressed and I tried to cheer her up. She finally smiled and got up and said, "Is soup all right?"

"Fine," I said, "and so is the cook." I got up and walked over behind her and put both arms around and hugged her while she worked.

"Be careful, Danny, I can only hold out so long."

"I love you so much, Gloria, I can wait till hell freezes over for you, if I have to. Just as long as I can hold on to you."

The soup was good and filling. We sat and talked about the events of the day.

"I can't believe Stephanie got to me like that," I said

"She was only trying to help, I don't think she was trying to open up any old wounds."

"When I walked out, it was just like being on the street again. I was just walking, going no place in particular. I was alone again, just walking the streets. My mind was in a daze, only this time I was sober. No pills, no booze, just bad memories, and suspicion. All the hurt and pain came flooding back. All the pain that you have taken away, came flooding back. That is why I got up and walked out. No man wants to believe he has been made a fool of. For a moment, I could see Mary and Artie doing things behind my back. I know that I no longer love her. I shouldn't even care what happened. It is just the way things occurred and the place I was. I was in the bush in Nam. My brother wrote to me and said that Mary didn't even bother to pick up the letters I wrote her. I never felt so helpless. I had no control over the situation. All I could do was let it happen."

Gloria got up and put her arms around me and said, "Let's go to bed and put this day behind us." I started out to my room and she pulled me into her bedroom.

"It is time we do things we have been putting off for too long. To hell with waiting for the wedding night." She took off all her clothes and stood there in the nude. I reached out and pulled her to me and kissed her.

I said, "Honey, you have the best body, and the worst timing in the world." She stood there naked with a puzzled look on her face. I said, "Gloria, where do you think they took the skin from to make me an eyelid?"

"You can't be serious!" she said.

"I'm sorry, but I'm afraid that's the way it is," I said.

She burst out laughing in that beautiful laugh of hers and said, "Danny, when the world gets you down, it kicks you square in the balls, doesn't it?"

I got undressed, except for a couple of bandages, and we slept together, our naked bodies entwined.

CHAPTER XIII

The world might have me down, I thought, but right now it Is not the world that I am trying to keep down. I still had stitches in places that arousal could cause some pain. I got up and washed up the best I could. I had to go back to the hospital and get the bandages changed, and hopefully some stitches removed. For I know someone who would try and have some fun at my expense.

We decided to call Mr. Black, the attorney, and talk with him if we could while we were in town. I still hadn't done anything with the settlement check. I knew I was losing money every day I held it, but when you haven't had money, it just doesn't seem to matter that much.

Gloria drove me to the hospital. I checked in and had to wait about an hour. So we spent the time in the cafeteria, drinking coffee and talking. She was teasing me about last night. Said if I hadn't been such a coward I could have ripped a stitch or two. I said, sure, with a little help, I could have removed them myself. We laughed and enjoyed each other's company.

Soon I was called in and the bandage changed. I got to talk a few minutes with Doc Carson. I invited him back to the farm. I told him I could use some help putting up the hay and that he need the exercise.

Then I thanked him for the warning about the skin graft on my eye.

"They didn't!" he said.

"I am afraid they did," I told him.

He laughed and said, "It will be a lot more fun winking now, Dan.

I said, "I got the stitches out today and it wasn't the eye."

We talked for a while. He said if he could get some free time, he would be out to see us. We went to the bank and I opened two cash deposit accounts for fifty grand each, putting Gloria on the accounts with me. I put the other forty thousand in my checking account. I needed to buy a car and then there would be the lawyer to pay.

We met with Mr. Black that afternoon, and he said I needed a copy of the birth records, and to get a copy of the divorce papers. We went by the department of motor vehicles and I got a copy of the driver's manual for me to study. I wanted to apply for a new license, but they wanted a copy of my birth record. They did give me a temporary license that I could drive with, as long as another driver was with me.

My new eyelid was starting to itch like crazy, so we went back over to the VA hospital and they gave me some ointment to put on it. We got home at about four. I changed clothes and told Gloria that I was going to finish baling before dark. She came out and rode the tractor with me for a couple rounds. I turned the baling over to her and started carrying bales and piling them about six or eight to a pile. That way if it rained so many of them wouldn't get wet, and they would be easier to pick up. She finished baling about seven and said she would go fix something to eat. I took the baler in and cleaned it up and serviced it; by then it was dark and I was starved.

Gloria was putting food on the table when I came in. I offered to help, but she said it was all done, just sit and eat. We sat and talked during the meal.

I said, "It will be Danielle's eighth birthday in two days and I am going to buy her something and take it to her."

"Do you think that is wise?" Gloria asked. "They may have a restraining order out on you."

"How would I know that?" I asked.

"We can make some calls in the morning. The police department can tell you."

After dinner, I went in and showered and went to bed. It had been a long day. Gloria came in later and lay down beside me. I put my arm around her and went back to sleep.

Morning came ever so quickly. After breakfast, Gloria drove the tractor and we piled hay in the barn all morning. After lunch I called the city police department and talked to Sergeant Pool.

I told him, "This is Danny Watts. I was supposed to call you several months ago, but just didn't get around to it."

He wanted to know about my meeting with Mary at the cemetery. He said, "She and Altie Johnson had filed a restraining order on you. That they feared you would do them bodily harm and try and take their little girl. That you claimed her as your daughter."

"She is my daughter!"

"Danny, that is for the courts to decide," he said.

"Can I buy her a birthday present and have it sent to her?"

"I wouldn't even do that without getting permission from a judge." I told him about the phone call I made to them a couple weeks ago. "They didn't say anything about a restraining order. Hell, they are trying to adopt Danielle."

He said, "Get a lawyer, Mr. Watts. You need one if you ever want to see that little girl."

Gloria and I were talking after I hung up. She asked me about Mary's folks. She asked me, "Does Mary have any family we could talk too?"

"Yes," I said. "Why hadn't I thought of them? God, how could I be so stupid? Her parents were real close to me. I loved them both. They only live a couple miles from here! I am going to call them."

I searched through the phone book until I found their number. Gloria was as excited as I was. Why in all my wandering and lying in hospitals hadn't I thought of Mr. and Mrs. Wilson! They had been as close to me as my real parents. I couldn't believe I have been in such a stupor all these years that I didn't think of them. I should have written to them when things went wrong with Mary and me. I guess self-pity can rob you of your senses. I was shaking, and mad at myself when I dialed the number. The restraining order couldn't keep me from talking to them.

The phone rang several times, and finally Mr. Wilson answered. I didn't know what to say. I finally said, "Hello! Mr. Wilson, this is Danny Watts."

There was a moment of silence on the other end.

Finally, he said, "Hello, son, how are you?" Then I heard him tell Mrs. Wilson that it is Danny.

She got on the phone and asked, "Where are you?"

"I am living just up the road, a couple of miles."

"We want to talk to you! May we come over?"

I told Gloria, "They want to come over." She asked, "When?"

"Right now, I think!" I told them how to get here and they said that they would be right over. I took a quick shower and cleaned up some. I wanted to look as good as possible, and for me that was hard to do. I still had a bandage over my left eye and the hair transplants hadn't been trimmed yet. I am a sorry-looking thing, I thought. I was as nervous as I could get. I needed a drink, so a soda had to do, as that was all we had.

It seemed like they would never get here. Finally, I saw their car coming up the drive. Gloria and I went out to meet them. There was the usual hugging and back slapping. I introduced them to Gloria and we all went inside and sat around the kitchen table. I offered them a soda, but they both said they would rather have coffee. Gloria poured them into each a cup. They asked me about my injury and I explained that I had been wounded. They didn't even know that! I explained how they were doing surgery on my eye, and hopefully I would be able to see out of it again.

Mrs. Wilson asked if I had seen Danielle. She said, "My how she has grown!"

I explained how I had never been allowed to see her. How I was thrown in jail the one time I tried, and how they had a restraining order against me, and the fact that Artie wanted to adopt her. Mrs. Wilson asked why I had abandoned them, that she thought I loved Mary. This really threw me for a spin. I said, "I guess there are two sides to every story."

I explained that Mary had quit writing me while I was in Nam. That after I was wounded, and in a hospital in Maryland, and my brother Vick had come to visit me and told me she had filed for divorce and was living with Artie. This brought tears to Mrs. Wilson 's eyes. Mr. Wilson just sat there in total silence. I explained how I lived on the street and it was nearly five years before I even knew Danielle's name. That I didn't find it out until Artie came to visit me in jail and asked to adopt her. Now I couldn't get a court order to see her because I couldn't prove she was my daughter.

Mr. Wilson asked, "Are you sure you want to do that? There is a lot of back child support to be paid."

I got a little angry, but I managed to keep my cool. I said, "I have paid child support ever since she was born. There has been two hundred and fifty dollars a month taken out of my check ever since I was discharged. And before that most all my military pay went to Mary, with an increase when the baby was born."

He just sat there and looked straight ahead. Finally, he said, "I guess you can prove that?"

I asked Gloria to bring me my pay stubs from my last check. I showed Mr. Wilson how I had been paying child support ever since I got a medical discharge.

"Danny," he said. "Something isn't right here, and I have felt it all along. We have been told a different story by Artie. He told us that you got strung out on drugs immediately after arriving in Viet Nam. That Mary quit hearing from you after she moved in with her sister, and how he would go by where you lived and there would be no mail."

I said, "Mr. Wilson, I wrote Mary every day that I could, clear up until the time that I was wounded and sent back to the states. My brother Vick can vouch for the fact that there were over twenty letters from me that were never picked up. He may still have them. I can find out."

"Artie also told us that you were kicked out of the Army for drugs and for being an alcoholic. That you came back to Springdale and were living on the street as a homeless person."

I said, "I did live on the streets. After paying child support, I couldn't afford to pay rent. I was hooked on prescription pain killers for a while, and I did drink a lot of wine just trying to forget the wrong that had been done to me and to try to keep from freezing to death on the street. I did go and try to see Danielle! Mary slammed the door in my face and called the sheriff. She said I looked too grotesque for Danielle to see, that I would scare her. That is when I tangled with the deputies and got thrown in jail. It wasn't for anything I ever said to Mary or Artie.

"The one and only time I have seen Danielle was at the cemetery when my mom died. I only got a brief look at her then! Mr. Wilson, this is all the truth as I know it. I would not lie to you. I loved Mary and it broke my heart when she divorced me. I couldn't understand, and I couldn't find her to talk to her. I have grown to hate Artie, who was once my best friend. I want to get Danielle something for her birthday! Would you give it to her for me? Due to the restraining order I can't go near them. Also, I need a copy of Danielle's birth record. Do you know if I am shown on it as her father?"

This all seemed to take them by surprise. Mr. Wilson got up and said, "It is getting late. Can we come back tomorrow?"

I thanked them for coming and said I would look forward to talking to them some more.

Gloria and I sat up and talked for a little longer. She said, "It sounds to me like Artie lied to those people."

"Yea," I said, "big time."

We went to bed, but I had too much on my mind to sleep very well. I lay there holding Gloria and thought, *was all this set up by Artie just to get Mary' away from me? Did he think I would die in Nam? Well, I almost did, but I am going to surprise that bastard yet. This is all going to come out in a court of law if it costs me every penny I have.*

The next morning I had to go back into the hospital and get my bandages changed and see when I had to go back to St. Louis. We checked in at the hospital. Then went to the cafeteria for breakfast while we waited for me to be called. Doc Carson had a few moments so he came down and had coffee with us. I told him about talking to Mary's parents.

He said, "Something doesn't sound right."

I was called up to outpatient treatment and Doc walked up with Gloria and me.

My bandages were changed and I was told to be in St. Louis in four days, as my eyelid had healed enough, they could start on my eye. When we got home, there was my birth certificate and a copy of my discharge in the mail, along with a copy of Danielle's birth record. I called the department of motor vehicles and got an appointment to take my driver's test the next day. I also called Mr. Black and said, "I have a copy of my daughter's birth record and I am shown as the father."

He said, "Excellent. I will file papers in court tomorrow to get visitation rights for you." I told him I had been unable to get a copy of the divorce papers. He said that it didn't matter, we would get them in court.

I was so excited that I wanted to celebrate. We called Mr. and Mrs. Wilson and asked them to meet us at the steak house for dinner. We waited at the diner for over an hour and the Wilsons didn't show, so we went in and ordered. We were half through the meal when Mr. Wilson came in. He said that Mrs. Wilson was too embarrassed to talk over dinner, that they would follow us home if we still had things to talk about.

"That would be fine," I said. We finished the meal and met them in the parking lot. They followed us home. Mrs. Wilson was very apologetic. She said, "I just can't talk about family matters where other ears are listening."

They both wanted to know about me. When was I wounded and how? And when Mary and I quit writing each to other. Mr. Wilson said he called Mary and she was very upset that they were even talking to me. He said that he told her he was going to get to the truth of the matter one way or the other. That he didn't believe all the stuff Artie had been telling them about me. Especially since he had talked to me.

Mrs. Wilson spoke up and said that she didn't trust Artie, that she thought he was abusive to Mary; she had shown up with too many bruises that couldn't be explained. She said, "I think Mary is scared to death of him. Danielle wouldn't go near him unless someone else was present.

"Danny, she was living with Artie before we ever knew anything was wrong. We knew that he was hanging around, but we just thought he was helping her for your sake. We never once thought that Mary would leave you.

"Then Artie started coming over to our house and telling us all this stuff about you being on drugs and being given an undesirable discharge from the Army. That you were living like a drunken beggar on the street."

I got up and walked over to the counter, picked up the new copy of my discharge papers and handed them to her.

She read the papers and said, "Well, this tells a different story! It says that you received three battle citations, two Purple Hearts, the Viet Nam combat medal, and the Silver Star, for extreme bravery under fire. That certainly doesn't sound like someone that was on drugs to me."

I asked if they knew that they had never told Danielle that I was her father.

Mrs. Wilson said, "I know she calls Artie daddy, but I just figured that was because he was taking the place of her father."

That one hurt! I told them that I had hired an attorney to try and get visitation rights, that I didn't want to take Danielle away from Mary. "All I want is to see my daughter, to be able to take her places, buy her things, and spend some time with her. I know for her sake this will have to be done gently, and over a long period of time. I am sure the courts will have some guidelines that we will have to follow." Mr. Wilson said, "It is getting late and we better get home."

Mrs. Wilson apologized again about dinner. I assured her that I understood and it was all right. We walked them out to their car and stood and watched as they drove away.

Gloria said, "I feel sorry for them. They are nice people and seem to be caught right in the middle of things."

I put my arms around her and apologized for getting her mixed up in my affairs.

She kissed me and said. "Danny! People in love share both good and bad. It doesn't matter whose side it is on, as long as we share. That is what love is all about. Family ties are built by two people, working and suffering together. Your problems, and my problems, are 'our' problems, and we will solve them together. If one of us stumbles the other is there to pick up."

I hugged her close to me and held her tight. "That's what I love about you, Gloria! Everything is always so simple."

She gave me a playful shove, and said, "Let's get to bed. We have work to do tomorrow."

We went to sleep holding each other tightly. We spent the next day just working around the farm. We had a call from Mr. Black that a Judge Scott had set our court date. It would be five weeks before all the papers could be served on everyone. I told Gloria that it should work out good. My eye surgery would be over with and we would have the next cutting of hay up by then.

Gloria drove me to St. Louis a day early. We toured the city. We went through the Arch and did the whole tourist bit. That evening we danced and partied at the hotel ballroom where we stayed. We both knew that this was going to be a very special night.

As we walked into the room, Gloria asked if I wanted to carry her across the threshold. I picked her up in one arm and lifted her across the doorway. She said, "Danny, I hope things still aren't sore. For they are going to be a lot sorer come morning."

We laughed, undressed and took a shower together. As we went to bed she said, "Danny, I want this to be our honeymoon night. Until we can have a real one!"

I pulled her to me, knowing it had been over eight years since I had had a woman.

CHAPTER XIV

The enjoyment of that night will remain burned into our memories for eternity. Gloria's husband had been gone for over three years and her desires were as strong as mine. We spent the morning caressing and loving each other. I had to report at one and Gloria still had a four-hour drive to get home. I had never felt so full of life. I wanted to forget the surgery and go home with her.

She dropped me off at the hospital and after saying a long goodbye. I stood and watched her drive away, thinking how I could ever be so lucky to find a person like her.

For the first time since I had been injured, I had a fear of the coming operation. I now had something to live for. Someone that wanted me! I signed in at the hospital and was given a pre-surgery checkup and prepped for the coming operation. I wasn't allowed to eat or drink anything that evening. It wasn't the first time I ever went to bed hungry.

Gloria called me that night and we talked for over an hour, not saying much, just casual conversation. I loved this woman and wanted to be with her. Maybe, with a little luck in a couple of months, I could become a normal person again, if there is such a person.

Dr. Peil came in the next morning and took the bandage off my eye, removed a couple stitches and asked me to try and open my eye. The eyelid would only open part way, and he told me that was normal, that I would have to build strength in it. I had to squint to get it shut.

The doctor told me to just try and wink, which worked pretty well.

He said, "I will see you in surgery, and hopefully when we're all done you will see me out of that eye."

They took me into surgery about one that afternoon. When I awoke the room was dark. There was a nurse sitting by my bed. She asked, "How do you feel?"

I said, "Like I have an eye full of sand, and my eye socket feels like you left someone in there."

She laughed, and said, "That is standard for a cornea transplant. The doctor will be in to see you pretty soon."

I lay there wondering what I will look like. I still didn't have much of an eyebrow, and there were no lashes on my eyelid. I guess I am lucky to have what I got. My hairline looked fairly natural now and my ear looked ok. I kept my hair long enough to cover most of it. This had been the most painful of all the surgeries.

Dr. Peil came in and discussed what had taken place. He said that there was more damage to the conjunctiva than he had expected, but he thought the cornea transplant would take all right. He said, "We will leave the bandage on for a couple of weeks, then have a look at it. You will have to stay in a dark room and remain fairly quiet for the first few days."

This was going to be pure hell on me for I had become very impatient in the last year. They gave me a sedative to help me sleep. Maybe I could sleep for the next two weeks, I thought.

Morning came and with it a splitting headache. They brought breakfast and I picked through it. I asked the nurse for something for the headache, so she had to check my medication and said it was probably caused from the sedative that they gave me the night before, and I should drink lots of liquids and it would go away in a little while. I asked if they had a radio that I could listen to. She said she would try and round one up for me.

I lay there thinking about all that had happened to me the past few years. I thought, what if Danielle didn't want anything to do with me? After all, I am just a stranger to her. How would I get involved in her life? How would she handle it when she found out Artie wasn't her father? Would this cause her to resent me?

It wasn't good to lay there in the dark and think. My mind had a hundred questions and I had none of the answers. Was Artie abusing Mary? Then the sickening fear hit me — what if he was abusing Danielle? Surely, Mary was a strong enough person not to let that happen. I was going nuts lying there!

Whatever came over Artie? He was such a good friend. Did he want Mary bad enough to lie to everyone in order to get her? I realized that my headache was gone. Maybe I wore it out wondering about so many things.

The nurse came in with a small radio and plugged it in. I found a talk show and listened to it until I was asleep. When I awoke it was early morning and the hospital was quiet. I lay there and listened to the sounds. I could hear people breathing and people moving around, and things rolling.

I thought back to my nights in Nam when we were on night patrol. Darkness brings with it, its own sounds, and I got to where I could hear the sound of fear from the men around me. I could listen and hear my own heartbeat. I heard other sounds in the night, even the sound of death. We would spend nights near burned-out villages that had dead bodies still lying around. Dead bodies make noises as the gases in them escape through the vocal cords. The most fearful sound in the night isn't made by an animal or insect, but by man. To hear the movement of the enemy, as he closes ground on you, and to know any moment you will have to fight for your own survival. Either kill or be killed.

The soft, crushing noise of grass being pressed down by a human foot, the unexpected quick breath a person takes, the changes of odors in the air. All of these things you learn to detect or you don't survive.

Most people never develop their animal instincts. Man has many senses that he never has to use so he doesn't learn them. In combat, the men that live learn to develop these, as well as improve on the ones he already uses. You must learn to read the signs that others leave behind. The broken stem of a weed, a turned over stick or leaf, a rock in a stream that has been stepped on and the silt washed off of it. All these things can give you the edge that you need to survive.

I thought of my first night in a listening post. The fear I had when the other post shot off the flare and started firing. Panic can get you killed. It can also make your pants awfully wet. You have to know what is coming in life and be ready for it. Now I know how I ended up homeless, and on the street. I didn't foresee it and I had never made use of my senses in case it did happen, but once there I learned to survive. I learned to feel people near me, even in my sleep. I could crawl under a home with everyone awake inside and hear their activity and never be discovered. I learned to never leave behind any sign of being there. I once left behind a wine bottle in a place that was warm and comfortable. The next time I went there to sleep it was boarded up to where I couldn't get in.

Morning finally came and with it the clanging and banging noises of people moving around. They brought me a tray of food. If you can call it that! Why is it that the dieticians in hospitals can't make one dish that tastes good? The food looks delicious but there isn't one bit of flavor in anything, but maybe the Jell-O, and it is hard to screw up Jell-o. I picked through my breakfast and ate a few bites. This stuff would have been hard to eat when I was starving on the street.

Gloria called about ten and we talked for over an hour. She had taken a gift over for Danielle and left it with Mary's folks. She had a good visit with them, and they wished me a speedy recovery.

My doctor came in and checked my eye. They kept me in a dark room to keep light out of my face. He removed the bandage and shined a damn light in my eye. I didn't only see light, I felt it clear to the back of my brain. I recoiled so quickly I almost went out of the bed backwards.

"Did you see anything?" he asked

"Yea," I said. "A light that went clear through my brain."

"Good," he said. He put a new bandage back on and told me he would be back to see me in a couple of days, and for me to stay out of the light.

They left me there alone in that dark gloomy room to listen to the radio and test my mind for sanity.

I thought about Gloria and the last night we had together, how good she was, and the smell of her hair and skin, her soft touch and the warmness of her body. I wanted out of here. I wanted her. Finally, the talk radio program came on and I listened to it for a couple hours then fell asleep.

They woke me up when they came in with the evening meal. The milk was cold and good and I had a dish of fresh apricots. They were delicious! It had been years since I had eaten apricots. The rest of the meal would have been eatable if I had some salt. When I got permission to walk around, I was going to go give that cook a box of salt and teach him how to use it.

I took a shower after dinner and sacked out. It was the first good night's sleep I had had since I arrived. Come morning I got up and sat in a chair. It was the most uncomfortable chair I ever sat in. I guess they make them that way so visitors won't stay too long. I thought to myself, Man! I have come a long ways. All the way from sleeping on the ground, to complaining about the food and the furniture. It just goes to show that mankind can't be happy no matter where he is. I have been here too long all ready, I need Gloria. I am going to ask if they allow congenial visits. Two more weeks in this place and I will be dingier than I was on the street after a four-day drunk.

I sat there for a while, then I finally I got up and walked around the room several times. I turned the radio on but there wasn't much to listen too. I hadn't heard any of the songs. I hadn't listened to music of any kind for so long, it is all new to me, and I didn't care for any of it. Once in awhile they would play some old song that I halfway remembered. I messed with the dial until I found a talk radio program. People were calling in and griping about the war, and everything from their car to their neighbor's dog. I finally lay down and slept for a couple hours.

When I awoke it was time for lunch. I had no appetite but thought I would lift the lid and see what kind of tasteless morsels they had dreamed up this time. One look and I ate the applesauce and drank the milk. The rest I covered back up and set the tray over by the door.

I lay back on the bed and shut my eye and tried to sleep. I thought about all the things I wanted to do on the farm. First thing I was going to do was get my driver's license. I had an appointment to take the test, and forgot to go take it. Then I wanted to buy a nice pickup. I ran all this through my mind several times.

Gloria called and I told her I was going stir crazy, for her to come up, and we could put a chair in front of the door or get in the closet. She laughed, and said, "You must be feeling better!" The attorney had called and everything was on schedule for the visitation hearing. I wanted to get that over with as quick as possible. We talked a little longer and she said that she would be up to see me on the weekend.

I was getting depressed. I hate that empty, lonely, sickening feeling that comes with it. What was the

HOMELESS

Ranger's creed? 'Fight harder, fight longer, fight smarter and fight quicker than anyone else.' It seems like I had been fighting longer than time itself, and I knew I had been fighting harder. I was just slow in starting this fight, and I didn't think I used any smarts at all, or I would have had all this behind me, and been living a normal life.

What would a Ranger do in my situation? Attack, always attack, and put your foe on the defensive as soon as possible. *Well, Mary and Artie, here I come and it is going to be a full-out attack. I intend to see my daughter. Even if I have to kick the damn door in and tell her who I am!* I was feeling better! Nothing like an appending attack to get the blood moving. *When that doctor gets here tomorrow, I am going to tell him, 'I need to get out of here. So figure out a way I can.*

Sleep came hard that night. How am I going to tell Danielle that I am her father? How will an eight-year-old girl handle it? Mary and Artie caused this mess but by God I am going to clean it up. As soon as I get home, I am going to consult a child physiologist about the problem. Fight smart. Have the answers before you get the problems. Don't procrastinate, be fast, do it now. Fight hard and bring in the big guns. Go to court with everything and everyone you need to win. Don't give up. Be prepared to fight as long as it takes. Wear them down. Wear them out. Know what your goals are. Have a plan. Know when you have won. Know when the battle is over. And most important, be ready to heal the wounded.

Morning finally came and I was really pumped. I even ate some of my breakfast. I showered the best I could and waited for the doctor. I had things to do, places to go and battles to fight.

I had walked around that room a hundred times. I even agreed with the talk show host a couple times. Doctor Peil came in about ten. He took my bandage off and helped me open my eye. I could see things. They were all fuzzy and blurred, but I could see things. He shined that damn light in my eye several times and that was painful. He asked if I could see colors. I really had to make my mind work.

"Yes." I was seeing reds, yellow and blue! He put some ointment into my eye and put the bandage back on it. I asked, "Can I leave the hospital now?"

"No! I am afraid not!" he said, "We have to start therapy tomorrow. You haven't been able to see out of that eye for several years. All the muscles and nerves that operate the iris, lens, and ciliary body have lain dormant. They have to be brought back to life and strengthened daily. This will be somewhat painful and will take two to three weeks. You can walk around the hospital, and you can open the drapes and let some light in. I will even let you watch some television, but not too much. Stay out of the sun and away from bright lights. I will be in to see you tomorrow and we will line up the daily therapy routine." Morning came and with it the doctor and the therapist. I had a whole series of eye exercises to do, from opening and shutting my eye to several sight procedures, consisting of looking at dimly colored lights to staring at one light for three minutes at a time. By the time this was over I was exhausted and had a terrible headache. This same procedure went on every day.

HOMELESS

Gloria came on Saturday and spent the day. We walked to the cafeteria for lunch and walked around the grounds. I wanted to be alone with her and to have her all to myself. She had to go back that evening so that left me in a depressed mood again.

My eye was improving fast. I could now leave the bandage off,

but had an extremely dark lens over it, with the glasses they had prescribed for me to wear. I had to constantly try and blink the eye. I learned to wink in order to close the eye. But things were getting stronger. I still had trouble opening the eyelid all the way. I worked hard at the exercises. I wanted to go home.

Two weeks finally went by and I was gaining sight pretty good in that eye. I looked in a mirror and was surprised. I looked halfway human again. I was released to outpatient status and told to come back every two weeks.

Gloria came to pick me up. I had to wear dark glasses and stay out of bright lights. She said, "I hope it stays cloudy so you can cut hay when we get home."

I told her I had other things planned for her when we got home.

She laughed and said, "I should have made you walk. That way you wouldn't be so full of energy."

CHAPTER XV

I was totally exhausted when we arrived home. My head ached and my eyes hurt. I went into the bedroom and laid down. How long I slept I don't know, but it was dark when Gloria came in and asked if I was hungry. I lay there awhile trying to get things straight. "Yes, I am," I said. "Hungry for you."

I grabbed her and pulled her down on the bed with me. We lay there and necked awhile. She got up and said, "Come on in the kitchen and I will fix us something to eat."

My appetite had returned and I was hungry. While we ate, I went through the phone book looking for a child physiologist. I wrote down a couple of numbers. Come morning I was going to make some phone calls. I was going to try for my driver's license, if I could take the test wearing the dark glasses. Also, I wanted to talk to the attorney. I wanted to know what he had planned to do, and who he was going to subpoena into court. I did not want for Danielle to have to come into a courtroom.

As evening came, Gloria and I walked hand in hand out through the hay field. It was ready to cut, and I wouldn't be able to help. I told her I would delay any meetings with anyone for a few days. I was going to call the child physiologist and talk to her. We walked around the farm and looked at the cattle. We discussed some of the things we wanted to do. The corn looked good. Overall everything was working out real good.

We walked back to the house as darkness fell. I was still tired, so we went to bed early. We lay there and talked as I held her close to me. I loved the smell of her hair and the feel of her warm body next to me. We drifted off to sleep lying there in each other's arms. It blew in a storm during the night with lots of thunder and lightning. This woke us up and Gloria got so close I thought she would push me out of bed. Being a warm-blooded man, I took advantage of the situation and we made mad passionate love the rest of the night.

We awoke to a cold, steady rain. There wouldn't be any hay cutting today. I called a Dr. Megan, who was a child physiologist, and was lucky enough to get an appointment that afternoon. I also called the department of motor vehicles and asked about taking my driver's test. After explaining about the surgery on my eye, they convinced me to wait until I found out how good my vision would be. We decided to go into town and do some much-needed shopping and see a few people.

I elected to drive. On the way, I got pulled over by a deputy for making a rolling stop. As luck would have it, no other than 'Deputy Hill' got out of the car and walked up to my window. I handed him my temporary permit. He failed to recognize me in the dark glasses, but one look at the picture on the permit, with the patch over my eye, got his attention real quick.

"Well, well, Mr. Watts. I wondered when we would meet again." I said, "I was hoping we would, for I want to apologize for what happened last time." He just stood there all braced and looking hard at me.

I said, "It wasn't you, sir, that I was striking out at that day. It was the whole damn world."

"That's funny, it felt just like it was me you hit." I asked if he had time for me to explain.

He said, "If it is good, I will wait."

I explained how I had just come back from Nam with my face shot up, and that my wife and best friend had moved in together, and I had never seen my daughter. I said, "All I wanted was to see that little girl! Instead, she slammed the door in my face and called you.

And you know the rest. I served forty days for that. I am truly sorry that ever happened. I lived on the street for several years, living like a bum. I got busted a couple times for being drunk. That was mostly for my own safety. Finally, I found out I could get some corrective surgery on my face. I have met this lady. We are getting married and we are in the process of trying to get visitation rights to see my daughter who is now eight years old. I have only seen her one time and that was from a distance. We are farming over four hundred acres just down the road here a couple miles. You are welcome to stop in anytime."

We talked for a while longer and he said, "It wasn't me that used mace on you. I knew about the reaction to burn tissue and the chemicals in mace. So I guess we all made some mistakes that night." He gave me back my permit and told me to come to a complete stop next time. I assured him I would and told him I meant it when I said for him to stop in anytime. He said he would and for me to take it easy.

We stopped and had a late breakfast. Did some shopping and went by the mission and saw Bob. He didn't recognize me with an ear and glasses, so I had a little fun with him, until he finally recognized my voice. We sat and talked for a couple hours. Then we drove over and met with Dr. Megan.

I explained the whole story to her and asked what kind of trauma she thought this would cause Danielle. She explained to me that kids are a lot tougher than we give them credit for. She said, "It will come as a shock to her probably. The best procedure would be for you to get acquainted as a friend. Then choose the right moment to tell her.

Dr. Megan assured me that the courts have adequate doctors that would guide us in the way to handle this. We drove over to see Vick and Sally. I thought we would take everyone out for pizza someplace.

Audrey, the youngest, opened the door when we knocked.

She said, "It's Uncle Danny and he has a new face."

We all laughed at this remark. Vick said, "Get in here, brother, and let's have a look at that new face."

Everyone was real interested in my eye and if I could see out of it. I had regained a lot of vision. I could make out most everyone, but things were still blurred. I have to go back in for stronger glasses in a week, I told them. Little Audrey wanted to know where my patch was. I had brought it in my pocket to give to her. I pulled it out of my pocket and put it on her eye. She looked like a little pirate, so I started calling her "Patch the Pirate." Rhonda and Kathy, the other two girls, wanted to try it on also. We all rode to the pizza parlor in Vick's car. It was quite a load, but a happy bunch. The pizza was good and the company was excellent. I told Gloria I wanted a family! She said, "Ok, but I think we should get married first."

I laughed and said, "Everything I want to do in life always has an obstacle jump in the way."

Vick laughed and said, "Well, that is just a minor one. When is the date set for?"

"We are waiting for the hearing to get over with." I asked him if he would be the best man and hold my hand.

He said, "Only if you start crying."

After the meal, we went back to Vick and Sally's and had a dish of ice cream for dessert. We visited for a while and then headed home. I turned to Gloria and said, "It is time we got married. Let's go get the license tomorrow!"

She said, "We have to cut hay tomorrow."

"Are you getting cold feet?"

"No! But you still don't have a copy of your divorce."

"I will get it when we apply for the license. We get it in the county clerk's office, so they should have a copy."

"We have to take you back to St. Louis in two days! We can get it then."

"You know, I think it would help if we were married when we ask for visitation rights. Things involving children go a lot smoother when a woman is involved."

She laughed and said, "Yes, I think it is easier to have them with a woman being involved."

"Well, lady!" I said. "When we get home, I am going to involve you in the process."

She laughed that cute giggle and said, "You are full of promises, Danny boy."

When we got home, we showered together. I took her to bed, wet hair and all. She smelled and tasted like a woman. I had thought I loved Mary, but there is no comparison to how much more I love Gloria. Mary was just a girl. Gloria was a full-grown woman, with a woman's needs, not just the hormonal lust like young girls have. Gloria knew how to please a man, how to make him feel like he was wanted. I tried to please her in every way I knew. I wanted to satisfy her every desire. I thought, God, I love this woman!

Morning came and I drove the tractor out into the hayfield and made a couple rounds with the swather. I had on a hat with a large brim on it, but I still wasn't supposed to be out in the sun. I felt like a damn fool sitting there in the shade while Gloria made round after round on the field. What if someone came by and saw me sitting there while she was working like that?

After a while I went into the house and fixed some iced tea. I gathered up some cookies and walked out to the field. We walked over to the shade of a big walnut tree and sat on the ground and had tea and cookies.

"I should have brought a blanket."

"Yes, and the hay would never get cut."

We sat and laughed. I finally got up and crawled up on the tractor and made several rounds while Gloria rested in the shade. I stopped and gave the tractor back to her. She kissed me and said, "I will expect supper about six."

Before I could answer, she had the tractor in gear and was moving. I walked back to the house, thinking, what can I cook? Hell, I don't know how to cook! And I am not supposed to drive without another licensed driver with me.

I went through every can in the kitchen and decided I could heat up some soup and make a grilled cheese sandwich without making too big a mess. I got everything ready and went back out in the yard with a glass of tea and sat and watched Gloria make rounds of the field.

I walked out to the mailbox. There was a notice from our attorney that they would start the hearing on Wednesday morning. I had to be in St. Louis Monday. This was Saturday. I began to get nervous again, and all of the "what ifs" began to cloud my mind. I was becoming worried. Could I handle being a father to an eight-year-old? What did I know about being a father? After all my planning, I wasn't prepared to win. I could become a casualty of my own making.

All of my Ranger planning was falling through. I could fight harder, smarter, longer and quicker, but what did it say about after you win. Man, I must have slept through that chapter"

I looked up and Gloria was coming through the gate. I got up and gave her a big hug. "Go wash up, I will have supper in a few minutes." I was ready. Where in the hell was the can opener? I used a knife like we did in the Army. I buttered the bread and put it in the skillet with the cheese in the middle, only I got the wrong side down. I poured the soup in a pan and added a can of water like it said, only I forgot to turn on the stove. Gloria came in and asked if she could help.

"No, I have everything under control."

She smiled and said, "Try turning on the right burners, things will get done a lot quicker." With that, she got up and straightened up the grilled cheese and heated the soup.

She said, "A person could starve to death waiting on you to cook something."

"Well, my intentions were good."

After we ate, she said, "What's for dessert?"

I jumped up and said, "Me!"

She just shook her head and said, "You need to work harder, Danny boy."

We both laughed and I said, "Well, I will do the dishes."

About that time she saw the soup can. "What on earth did you use to open that with? Your teeth?"

"I couldn't find the can opener."

She got up and took me by the hand and led me over to the cabinet by the sink and pointed to some gizmo. "This, Danny boy, is a can opener."

"Well! Mom always kept it in the drawer."

She smiled and said, "Mom doesn't live here."

I knew when I was beat, so I picked this opportunity to shut up.

We went to bed early as we were both tired, she from work, and me from stress. That cooking can be hell on a person!

Come morning, we decided to go to church. Now I hadn't been in a church since I was a teenager. Gloria thought it would help our cause if we had a preacher on our side. The church was a little country church that had maybe forty people attending. Gloria seemed to know everyone, including the preacher. She introduced me to everyone as her intended. Everyone congratulated us and wanted to be invited to the wedding. The service was a long affair that put your mind to thinking. Man! I had a lot to answer for.

I sure hoped there was forgiveness somewhere. After the service, we stayed around and talked to the preacher and some other farmer. Mostly about hay and the weather.

After we got home, I changed clothes while Gloria fixed lunch. She didn't want to chance it with me again!

I changed the swather for the baler, and put new twine in it, and after lunch I baled several rounds of the field. Gloria came out and stopped me and told me I better get into the shade. I was sitting there watching her when Doc Carson and his girlfriend drove up. I walked out to greet them.

He introduced his girlfriend Sarah and asked, "Where is Gloria?" I pointed toward the hay field. He laughed and said, "Man, you know how to train them right." This brought a playful slap from Sarah. "How is the eye doing?" he asked.

I removed the glasses. He looked real close at it, and said, "Looks a little cock-eyed to me." We both laughed and Sarah stood there with a puzzled look on her face.

I said, "Don't explain it! She will want a closer look." We both laughed harder.

Doc said, "I will explain later."

Gloria saw them and came in from the field. I introduced her to Sarah and she invited everyone in. Doc said, "I came out here to work. What do you want me to do?"

"Just sit and visit is all. We are mostly caught up."

"Don't look that way to me," Doc said. "I know how to run a baler. Come on, show me how to get started."

We talked as we walked out to the field. He was trying to decide if he wanted to specialize in one certain type of medicine or be a general practitioner. I explained I had to get out of the sun. He fired up the tractor and said, "Better follow the doctor's orders."

I walked back to the shade and sat down, feeling guilty and lucky at the same time to have such a good friend! I hoped that he would stay around Springdale. It was a great place to live. He finished the baling in about two hours and wanted to help pile bales. I told him he was asking for punishment. I unhooked the baler and hooked up the wagon. He told me if I covered the eye I could help.

"Thanks a lot! Just when I had it all going my way."

He got some gauze out of a bag he had in his car and wrapped up my eye. Gloria came out and drove the tractor. Sarah and I rode the wagon and stacked bales as Doc pitched them on for us. We worked until almost dark. I finally made everyone quit.

We walked back to the house and had some iced tea and cookies. I thanked Doc and Sarah for the help. They got up to leave and I told him to think about staying around here, that we always needed a good doctor and I needed him and that I didn't save his butt so that he could work in some New York hospital. He laughed and said they would be back as soon as he could get a day free. We walked them to the car and said goodbye.

As they drove away, I turned to Gloria and said, "They are nice people."

"Danny, the world is full of nice people, and don't you forget it."

CHAPTER XVI

The trip to St. Louis was uneventful. My eye was healing well. I was still having some trouble with the eyelid sagging, but Doctor Peil assured me if I kept exercising it that it would get strong enough so that I could hold it open naturally. He prescribed me a lighter tint on the glasses and said I could take a little more sun now, but to keep it shaded with a hat brim. They gave me a patch for my good eye and told me to wear it at least a couple of hours a day, that I had to work my weak eye too, to make it stronger!

We hurried back to the farm as we still had some hay to pile in the barn, and the hearing for my visitation was the day after tomorrow. It was late by the time we reached home, so we went to bed and got ready for a new day.

Morning came all too swiftly. After a quick breakfast, we headed for the field. Gloria drove while I piled bales on the wagon, stopping ever so often so I could climb on and stack them straight. We finished up the field about noon. I showered while Gloria fixed lunch. After we ate, Gloria bathed and we headed for the courthouse to get our marriage license.

On the way, we stopped and talked to the preacher of the little church we had attended on Sunday. We asked if he would do the honors and if we could have the wedding in his church. He said it would be a pleasure to marry us. We also told him about the hearing tomorrow and asked if he would have time to come and put in a good word for us. We explained the whole thing to him and he assured us he would be there.

The county clerk's office was crowded when we arrived. We had to sit and wait for almost an hour. We filled out the application for a marriage license while the clerk looked for my divorce records. The clerk came back and informed us that they had no record of a divorce, but that it could have been filed in another county. She said that a lot of people did that to keep it out of the local papers.

She issued us a marriage license and told us to be sure about the divorce in order to save us problems later on. I really wasn't concerned with it. I would just ask Mary tomorrow at the hearing. We stopped at the roadhouse on hwy. 44 and ate supper. I didn't have much of an appetite. I was starting to worry about the hearing. Sometimes I think life on the street was a whole lot simpler. All I had to do was worried about staying warm and eating, or getting arrested, or getting beaten up! Or dying out there in the cold! I guess it wasn't so good after all.

We came home and relaxed, or at least tried too. I could tell that Gloria was getting a little nervous about the pending trial. I walked over to where she was lying on the couch and knelt down and kissed her. She kissed back and the next thing I knew we were both on the floor. We took our pleasures with each other, then lay there and talked until we both fell asleep. I finally awoke and told Gloria to get up and come to bed. I don't think she ever fully woke up. Then I couldn't sleep for thinking about tomorrow. My mind went through everything I could remember that might make me look like an unfit father. What kind of stories would Mary or Artie tell? I had always been a fighter, but this time I didn't know where to begin.

Doc had told me to walk a wide circle around her. What did he mean by that? I finally drifted off to sleep and morning was there before I was ready. I got up and showered and went over all the notes the attorney had given me on what to do and what not to do. "By all means," he said, "don't let them make you angry. If they do, don't let it show."

Gloria came in and fixed breakfast. I really wasn't hungry but tried to eat anyway. The coffee tasted good. We talked about what to wear. I decided to just wear jeans and a sport shirt. I had never been a fancy dresser, so why start now?

We arrived at the courthouse an hour early and sat in the car and talked until I saw our attorney arrive. We walked over to meet him. He smiled and said, "Good morning." He told me not to be nervous. I said, "That's easy for you to say, I don't spend much time in court."

He assured me everything would be ok. We went in and took our seats at the table up front.

I looked around and Mary's parents were there, also my brother Vick and Sally, the preacher from church and several people I had never seen before. Mary came in with her attorney. I didn't see Artie anywhere.

Judge Scott came in and we were called to rise. Then he told us to be seated. The court clerk read the case number and stated it was for joint custody of one minor child. I hadn't asked for joint custody, so I asked my attorney about it. He said, "Don't worry, it was just legal terms." I was so damn nervous and my mouth was so dry, I doubted if I could talk if I had too.

I looked at Mary. The once beautiful girl I had married was pale and drawn. Her face looked puffy and she looked like she had been crying. I wanted to go put my arms around her and tell her everything would be all right. I thought, I must be nuts! This is the person that has kept your daughter from you for over eight years, and you are feeling sorry for her!

Gloria must have been reading my mind. She reached over and squeezed my hand. The attorneys got up and each one explained his case. Mary's attorney said that I deserted the family when Danielle was a baby, and that I had no legal rights to ask for visitation privileges or joint custody! That I chose to live like a bum on the streets of Springdale rather than be a father to my daughter.

I could see this was going to turn into a real dog and pony show. I felt better after my attorney gave his opening summation. He told how I went into the Army to serve my country, that I came back badly disfigured, and my wife told me I was too ugly to see my daughter, that he could prove I tried to see my child and was turned away by Mary. That she had called the police, and I had been arrested and thrown in jail just for trying to see my daughter. That I went for five years not even knowing her name.

I turned and looked at Mary; she was crying. I didn't know how much of this I could take.

They called Mary to the stand first. Her attorney asked her to tell about the night she had me arrested. She told how I came to the house without being invited and pounded on the door. That I was drunk and threatened to kick the door in if she didn't open it! That I attacked the first officer that arrived! That she feared for the officer's safety, and she called again, to get help for him. That it took three officers and a dog to subdue me. That she feared for her safety and Danielle's safety.

I felt that I was going back to jail. I didn't have a chance after her testimony. I sure didn't remember it like she told it. I didn't believe the police dog ever got out of the car. I wasn't drunk. Maybe I had a drink or two in me to calm my nerves. Wish to hell I had one now!

Then she told about the meeting at the cemetery, how I threatened Artie and said I would come take Danielle. That they put out a restraining order against me for their own safety. I couldn't remember ever threatening anyone. Why would she stretch the facts like that? Where was Artie?

It was my attorney's turn to ask some questions. He asked her, "Mrs. Watts, why are you still using Danny Watts' last name? Isn't your current husband's name Artie Johnson?"

"No, he isn't my husband."

Mr. Black said, "Would you explain this to the court?"

She said, "Artie and I have never gotten married! Legally I am still married to Danny."

I could have fallen through the floor. Gloria had tears in her eyes. I tried not to show my anger or surprise. I could feel everyone in the courtroom looking at me. Even my attorney, Mr. Black, was taken aback by this.

He asked, "Did you or did you not file for divorce when your husband was in Viet Nam?"

"Yes. I did file for a divorce! But Artie talked me into putting it off. He said that if Danny got killed over there, that we would get his life insurance money! After we found out he had been shot, we thought that he might not live, so I never went through with it."

"Mrs. Watts. When did you stop writing to your husband?"

"It was shortly after he went to Viet Nam. He just quit writing to me. I wrote every day and never got a word back."

"Mrs. Watts, are you aware that there are twenty-two letters that were mailed to you, at your and Danny's address? They were never picked up. All post marked several months apart."

Her attorney objected and said those so-called letters are just hear-say.

Mr. Black pulled the stack of letters out of his brief case and asked to have them entered as evidence.

Mary said that Artie went by their old place several times a week, and there had been no mail delivered, and that she gave Artie letters to mail to me every day for three months! Long after I had quit writing to her. That she had mailed me over a dozen pictures of Danielle, with her name and age on each one.

I was starting to get the picture of what went on. I sat there and held Gloria's hand. Mary would not make eye contact with me. Why did all this have to be drug out? Why couldn't they just let me visit Danielle? It wasn't like I was going to take her away from them. I wanted to stop this now. There had to be a better way. I felt sorry for

Mary. She looked so small and scared sitting up there all alone. I just wanted to sit down with her and talk to her.

Finally, Mr. Black said he had no further questions, but that he wanted to subpoena Artie Johnson. They called a brief recess. When we reconvened, Officer Hill took the stand. Mary's attorney asked him to tell of the night in question, when he and other officers had to arrest me. He said that I was very upset and that I had been drinking. However, he didn't think I was intoxicated. That I had put up a fight and they used mace on me, and that I was injured by the mace, due to new burn tissue that wasn't completely healed.

"Do you believe that Danny Watts is a dangerous person?"

"No, sir, I do not. He had some problems back then, that I believe was caused by the war, and his treatment by society after he returned." There were no more questions of him by Mary's lawyer.

Mr. Black asked if he had any contact with me since then.

"Yes," he said. "I had an occasion to stop Mr. Watts a few weeks ago for a minor traffic infraction."

"Would you tell the court what happened?"

"I told him, 'So we meet again.' Mr. Watts said he was hoping we would, as he wanted to apologize for striking me that night. He apologized twice, I believe, and even invited me to visit his home. "Thank you, Officer Hill, there will be no further questions." He was dismissed.

Mary's sister was called to the stand. She testified that she had seen Mary write letters to me, long after she had quit hearing from me, that Mary was very upset and even tried to get the military to contact Danny.

Mr. Black asked, "Did you see Mrs. Watts mail those letters?"

"No," she said. "She always gave them to Artie to mail."

With that she was dismissed and we went into recess until the following day.

The next day, court convened and a very nervous Artie Johnson took the stand.

Mr. Black asked him, "Did you pick up all the mail for Mrs. Watts at her old address?" He said, "Yes, I did."

"Mr. Johnson, are you aware of the penalties of perjury?" "Yes, sir," he answered.

Mr. Black said, "Let me remind you that you are under oath." He reached over and picked up the stack of unopened letters and asked him again, "Did you, to the best of your knowledge, pick up all the mail at that address?"

Artie turned a sickly white color and finally said, "I got tired of going by there, so I quit picking it up."

The next question from Mr. Black was, "What did you do with all the letters that Mary gave you to mail to her husband?"

Artie knew that he had been had, but really didn't seem to care all of a sudden. He looked straight at me and said, "I threw them in the trash at work. Danny didn't deserve to have her. If he really cared for her, he would have stayed out of the Army."

Mr. Black asked, "Mr. Johnson, whose idea was it to adopt Danielle?"

He said, "That was all Mary's doing. I told her that the minute I adopted her all the child support checks would stop, and that I wasn't going to support someone else's kid!"

"No further questions, Mr. Johnson, you may be excused."

After a brief recess, I was called to the stand. Mr. Black asked me to tell the court my story.

"I really don't know where to start, so I'll sort of go from the beginning," I said. "We were married right after high school. I got drafted and sent to Viet Nam. I had been in that country for about six months when I got wounded in the face. I lost most of my left ear and was blinded in my left eye. I was burned badly on that side of my face. While I was in the hospital, my brother came and told me my wife had moved in with my best friend, and that I had had a little girl! I never learned her name until she was nearly five years old. I got a medical discharge from the Army and a small pension. I have paid two hundred and fifty dollars every month to Mary for child support.

"I couldn't afford to eat and rent a place to live. So I ended up homeless, living day to day on the street. All I want is to be able to see my daughter. I now have a home and I am getting ready to remarry. I just want to get to know my child, and for her to know who her father is. I am not asking for custody of her, but I would like to have it. All I want is to help raise my daughter. Is that asking so terribly much I couldn't help it, but I broke down and cried there in front of everyone. The stress of this had finally broken me. The courtroom got real quiet. Mr. Black said, "That will be all." And the judge told me I could be excused. I wanted to run out of there. I looked at Gloria and she was crying. Mary and her folks were crying. Even Mary's attorney sat with a solemn face. Altie sat there with a smirk on his face like he didn't give a damn about anything or anyone.

All of a sudden, anger hit me I wanted a piece of that bastard in the worst way. Only I didn't want to jeopardize my chances of getting to see my daughter. I gave him a cold hard look and he got the message. The smirk came off his face and a look of fear filled his eyes. I had seen this look in men's eyes in Nam during battle and just before we went into combat. He knew he had made an enemy. One that would somehow even the score! I tried not to show my anger as I sat there.

Gloria reached over and grasp my hand. I wrote on a piece of paper, lam ok. I love you. She squeezed my hand again. Both attorneys wound up the proceedings with the why and why not of it all. Judge Scott said he would review the proceedings and make a ruling in three days, that only the parents and the child in question could be present, along with both attorneys.

After the judge left, we all stood up to leave when Mary started over to talk to me, and Artie grabbed her arm and pulled her back. I started for him and Gloria and my attorney both grabbed me. "No, Danny. Don't wreck things. It isn't worth it."

I needed to get out of there. I was a total wreck.

For three days I worked around the farm harder than I had ever worked before. I tried to keep my mind off things. I didn't even bother Gloria. Court time came and Gloria drove me in. I went into the judge's chamber and there sat

Mary and Danielle. I sat down and Judge Scott asked Mary how much the child knew about me.

Before Mary could answer, Danielle spoke up and said, "I know he is my daddy." My heart stopped beating for a few seconds. She said, "1 heard Mommy and Daddy talking at the cemetery the day we seen you. That's when you had the patch over your eye."

Judge Scott spoke up and said, "Well, that solves the problem of how we are going to tell her. Mrs. Watts, you are going to have some explaining to do to her. I am going to give you joint custody of Danielle, and I don't want to see you in my court again.

"Mr. Watts, I would finalize that divorce as soon as possible. Come see me with the papers and I will handle it for you."

Mary stood up and said, "Danny, I am so sorry. I really let Artie lead me down a wrong path. I know you must hate me for this."

"I don't hate anyone, but you robbed me of eight years of my daughter's life. How can you ever pay that back? And don't tell me it was Artie. You are stronger than that. You should have let me see her that day; I don't care how bad I looked. Do you have any idea how much nerve it took for me to come there?

"It took me several years to find you. If you want to know how I suffered just go spend one night walking the streets. Trying to hide from people and wanting someone to talk to at the same time. I just wish everyone could spend one week as a homeless person and try to survive on the street. It would change a lot of people's minds about things."

The judge said we had some papers to sign with the court clerk. He wished us both well, and then he told Danielle to be good to her mom and daddy.

I took her by the hand and looked into her eyes and said, "You know, I love you very much!"

She smiled and put both arms around my neck, and said, "Daddy, I love you too."

CHAPTER XVII

Judge Scott stated that he wanted to talk to both Mary and me in private, so the clerk took Danielle out to the front office.

"Mr. Watts. I can see a lot of anger and resentment in you, and I am worried that we might see you here again. I want to warn you that I will not tolerate you taking revenge on Mary or Artie Johnson. I have handled many of these proceedings before and have seen how a lot of them turn out. So whatever you are planning in retaliation, let me tell you: Forget it!

"Mary, I know that you are planning on trying to get some of the settlement that Mr. Watts got from the county. I don't have any authority in that matter, but let me warn you, this can only draw you two further apart and hurt your child. I doubt that you can get one penny, being that this all took place after you moved out of the home Danny had supplied for you and your daughter.

"To avoid further conflict between you two, the court has made arrangements for any meetings between Danielle and her father to go between the grandparents, Mr. and Mrs. Wilson.

"I want both of you to pay heed to my words: Put this all behind you and get on with your lives and do everything that is possible to raise your daughter to be a well-adjusted child. If either of you have anything to say to the other, do it here and now, and get it over with! "Mr. Watts, you may go first."

I really didn't know where to start or what to say. I told Mary that I could never forgive her for all the hurt she had put me through. "Especially the part of taking up with Artie. Who had been my best friend! I do understand his part in causing us to grow apart, but you were a strong enough person that you could have resisted him if you had wanted too. You have no idea the pain and suffering you put me through. Especially while I was in Nam. I tried to get myself killed on account of you. I walked these cold, lonely streets thinking of you. You were in the bottom of every bottle of wine I drank. All my anger toward society was aimed at you. So you go back to 'Dear Old Artie' and live happily. I have found someone I love very much, and someone that respects me for who I am, not for what I look like! But that is something you can never understand. Really! I never want to see you again. So go and do your thing and be happy.

"That's all I have to say, sir."

The judge then asked Mary if she had anything to say. All she said was, "Danny, I truly loved you. I never meant to hurt you, and I am so sorry. I should never have let Artie talk me into the things he did. He is no good and I am leaving him. So goodbye, Danny, I will always care for you."

Like the damn fool I am, I put my arm around her and told her everything would work out. "I will try to forget and forgive. Let's never show resentment for each other in front of Danielle."

With that said, we went into the judge's office and signed papers for joint custody.

I was visibly shaken by the whole proceeding. I scarcely said a word to Gloria on the drive home. I busied myself around the farm for the next few days, just dreaming of the coming week when I would have Danielle for three whole days.

Gloria and I planned a full weekend for her. We were overcome with happiness. I didn't know what to do first. This was Wednesday and we would get her Friday night. The Wilsons were to bring her over. I couldn't keep my mind on the farm work. Several things didn't get done because of my daydreaming. I had waited for so long to be with my daughter and now the time was near.

It was Friday morning and I was mowing the third cutting of alfalfa. I had about half the field cut when I saw the county sheriff's car pull into the farm. I figured Officer Hill had finally decided to stop for a visit. I shut the swather down and walked to the house. I needed a cold drink anyway.

I greeted Officer Hill with a handshake and told him it was about time he had decided to pay us a visit.

He said, "Danny, I am here on official business. I need to talk to you and the missus if I may."

I invited him into the kitchen. We sat down, and Gloria fixed us both a cold glass of tea. I asked him what this was all about.

He said, "It's about your wife Mary. She was found by her sister this morning lying in a pool of blood. She had been severely beaten.

She is still unconscious and is in intensive care at the city hospital."

"Where is my daughter?" I asked.

"We thought you might be able to tell us that."

"Why would I know that? I don't get to visit her until Friday."

"Would you mind coming to the office with me and answering some questions? You are not a suspect as yet, but we have to cover all bases."

"I just want to find my daughter," I said. "I will do anything I can to help."

We followed Officer Hill to the sheriff's office. I was so upset that Gloria wouldn't let me drive. A thousand things went through my mind, and they all turned up at Artie's door. That bastard was as worthless as the tits on a boar hog. If he had hurt Danielle, I would make a shoat out of him and enjoy doing it.

At the sheriff's office we were introduced to a Detective Bailey. He had been assigned to the case. He told us as much as he could then started asking me questions, about where I had been the night before and this morning.

I asked if I was a suspect. He said yes, and advised me of my rights.

I told him I had been on the farm all the time and Gloria could vouch for that.

He said, "She isn't a reliable witness." Which really pissed me off, and he knew it!

"Let me explain! Wife and girlfriends don't make for good alibis. The court doesn't believe they are reliable, due to the live-in situation, but they are better than nothing."

I asked if I was going to be held.

He said, not at this time, but for me to stay in the area. If I decided to go out of the state, I was to notify them before leaving.

I told him that Artie did it, and they should be looking for him, not me.

He said that Artie was a suspect, and they were looking for him. I asked, "What about Danielle! Where is she?" "We are looking for her too," he said.

"You damn sure better be, and you better find Artie before I do." "Mr. Watts, you keep talking like that, and we will lock you up."

I apologized and asked if we could leave. He said, "If you hear from Mr. Johnson or your daughter, call me immediately!" I knew that Artie had taken Danielle. But where?

His folks had a cabin down on Bull Shoals Lake in Arkansas. We used to stay down there and fish when we were kids. Could he have taken Danielle down there? I had to find him and my daughter. I called Detective Bailey and asked if they would search the cabin. He said they didn't have jurisdiction in Arkansas. I told him to call the FBI, that this was kidnapping. She wasn't his daughter and he had no custody rights to her. He informed me that they were investigating every lead, and it was only a matter of time until they found her and Artie.

I said, "At least call the Arkansas authorities and have them check the cabin!"

We drove home, both of us in our own somber mood. I couldn't eat because I was worrying about Danielle. I finally told Gloria to pack some clothes, we were going to

Arkansas. "If the damn cops are too lazy to look for them, then I will do it for them."

I didn't know if I could even find the cabin, but I had an idea where to look. We had to feed and water the livestock before we left, so we decided to wait until the next morning to leave.

I tossed and turned all night. Finally, we got up about four and we were on the road by five. It was a couple hours' drive from Springdale down route 65, and then over to 14. From there we had to go toward Diamond City off of route 7. There were so many winding roads around the lake, I knew that I would have trouble finding the right one. We drove around the lake area for a couple hours. I must have driven past the turn off into the cabin several times before I decided to try it.

We drove up this dirt road for about a mile past several cabins. Then there it was, and Danielle was standing on the porch. I stopped the truck, jumped out, and called her name.

At first, she just stood there. Finally recognizing me, she came running to me. I held her close, and then Artie showed up in the doorway. I handed Danielle to Gloria and told her to go get the police. Artie turned to get back into the cabin. I took after him like a pit bull after a cat. He started pleading and begging me not to hurt him. I held off for a while, then common sense overcame me, and I hit the bastard in the face with all I could muster. I drug him out onto the porch and made him sit in a chair until Gloria got back with the police.

When the police arrived, Artie got brave and his mouth was going a mile a minute. He accused me of everything he could think of. I explained to the Arkansas State trooper what had taken place, leaving out the part about slapping dear old Artie around some. We all had to go to the state police headquarters. One call to Detective Bailey and things began to move.

The cops asked Danielle about her mother, and she told them that Artie had beaten her and her mother, that he had made her undress and get in bed with him, and that he had touched her in places that he shouldn't. I wanted a piece of that bastard so bad I could have whipped every cop on the force to get to him. I managed to keep my cool and let the law handle it.

Artie was in deep shit, and we all knew it. Maybe life wasn't so bad after all. Child molesting, and kidnapping, plus taking a minor child across state lines without permission, he was looking at doing some serious time. He was also facing assault and battery charges in Missouri. At last he was going to get his and I was going to do everything I could to help.

We took Danielle home with us. It had been a very trying experience for her. She was very concerned about her mother, so we went directly to the hospital. Mary was still unconscious and in intensive care, so we were not allowed to see her. We took Danielle down to the cafeteria and tried to get her to eat. She drank part of a glass of milk and nibbled at her sandwich. Gloria wrapped it up for her in a napkin and let her take it with her. We stayed at the hospital several hours then took Danielle home with us. She was exhausted and went to sleep as soon as we put her to bed.

HOMELESS

I was beat and the hot shower felt good. I finally had my daughter at home with me after nine long years. It wasn't like I wanted things to be, but she was here! For how long I didn't know, but I planned to make the most of it. I went to sleep smiling for the first time in years.

Morning came quickly and Danielle was up early and followed me around the farm as I did the chores. She must have asked a million questions, which I was glad to answer. We called the hospital as soon as we got back to the house. Mary had regained conscious but was still in critical condition. We would not be allowed to see her for some time yet.

I called Detective Bailey, and Artie had been brought back to the county jail, even though the Arkansas authorities had charges pending on him. Bailey chewed my butt for not telling him I was going to Arkansas.

I said, "Hell, someone had to do it for you guys! Artie would be in Mexico by now if I hadn't gone after him."

He thanked me and said if I had given him better directions to the cabin they would have found him first. He wanted to know how Artie's face got messed up.

I said, "It must have been when he ran into the screen door as we drove up."

"Yea!" he said. "A two-hundred-and-twenty-pound screen door." We both laughed and he said he would let us know when the court date was set for Artie. I thanked him and hung up.

Gloria had breakfast fixed and I ate breakfast with my daughter for the first time. We went fishing down at the pond. It was the first time she had ever been fishing. The little blue gill were biting good and we caught a lot of them. Gloria caught a nice bass. I wanted to keep it, but she made me turn it loose. It was the most fun I have had in ten years.

When we got back to the house, Mr. and Mrs. Wilson were there. They had been up to see Mary but were only allowed to look in through the door. We decided to have a barbeque for lunch, and I drug out the ice cream freezer. Mr. Wilson and Danielle turned the crank on the freezer, while I cooked the burgers. Gloria and Mrs. Wilson had become great friends. They got along like mother and daughter. I could hear them talking in the kitchen. It seemed a shame that Mary couldn't somehow fit into all of this, but she made her choice, so I guess she would have to live with it. We enjoyed the meal and talked until late in the evening.

We called the hospital and were told that we could see Mary for a couple of moments the next day. I tried to prepare Danielle for the shock of seeing her mother swollen, bruised and in bandages.

We got to the hospital about ten the next day. Even I wasn't prepared for the shape Mary was in. They only let us look in from the door. Danielle was allowed to walk in and hold her hand for a moment. It is a wonder that she wasn't killed from the beating she had taken. I wish I had given more to Artie while I had had the chance.

Danielle was in tears when we left. She kept saying, "I tried to make him stop, but he just kept hitting her. Daddy, I never want to see him again."

I assured her that he would never harm her or her mother again. That she was my little girl and I would always take care of her.

Judge Scott called, and he had granted my divorce. Mary hadn't contested any of it. I guess that is why Artie beat her. He wanted part of the settlement money I had gotten from the county, and Mary knew it would go to educate Danielle.

The next few days went by swiftly, with daily visits to the hospital.

Mary was healing fast and finally she was strong enough to talk to us. She asked me if I would take care of Danielle. I assured her I would and that she could come visit her anytime she wanted. She cried and said what a mess she had made of her life and Danielle's. I told her she was young enough to make a fresh start, and she still had her parents to rely on, that she would not end up on the street homeless.

Detective Bailey called to tell us that Artie had pled guilty to all charges and that a sentencing date had been set for the following week.

I spent the next week harvesting the corn, with Danielle driving the tractor, with me sitting behind her. She loved being out in the field and was good with the cattle. Gloria and I planned the wedding for the following Sunday at the little church we attended, It wasn't to be a big affair, just a few friends and family.

Sunday came and I was a bundle of nerves. My brother Vick was the best man and his wife was the maid of honor, with Danielle being the bride's maid. My knees shook so hard I didn't think I would make it. There has to be a better way, at least for the groom. Anyway, we made it through and had a reception at the farm.

Danielle stayed with the Wilsons so she could go see her mother each day, while we took a quick honeymoon trip to Branson. I wanted to be back for the sentencing date on Thursday.

The courtroom was packed. The district attorney even had Mary there in a wheel chair. One look at her and I knew Artie was going to get his. The judge asked a few questions, and the DA presented his case. Artie had pled guilty to assault and battery, sexual child abuse, and to leaving the state to avoid prosecution.

The judge told Artie about the seriousness of the charges he had pled guilty to. He asked him if he understood his rights. He nodded and said, "Yes, I do."

The judge gave him seventeen years, without a chance for parole until he had served at least ten years. He also forbid him from ever having contact with Danielle or Mary in the future.

Artie stood there white as a ghost. I almost felt sorry for the bastard for a moment or two. I guess I always was for the underdog.

As we left the courtroom, I walked up to Artie and I said, "Artie, they love blond-headed boys where you are going. Enjoy yourself!

www.ingramcontent.com/pod-product-compliance
Lightning Source LLC
LaVergne TN
LVHW040140080526
838202LV00042B/2975